# THE TAKE
# DOWN

An Urban Novel written

LATIFA AYYUBI

*The Take Down*

Copyright © 2019 by Latifa Ayyubi. All rights reserved.

No part of this publication may be reproduced, stored in a retrieval system or transmitted in any way by any means, electronic, mechanical, photocopy, recording or otherwise without the prior permission of the author except as provided by USA copyright law.

This novel is a work of fiction. Names, descriptions, entities, and incidents included in the story are products of the author's imagination. Any resemblance to actual persons, events, and entities is entirely coincidental.

The opinions expressed by the author are not necessarily those of URLink Print and Media.

1603 Capitol Ave., Suite 310 Cheyenne, Wyoming USA 82001
1-888-980-6523 | admin@urlinkpublishing.com

URLink Print and Media is committed to excellence in the publishing industry.

Book design copyright © 2019 by URLink Print and Media. All rights reserved.

Published in the United States of America
ISBN 978-1-64367-294-6 (Paperback)
ISBN 978-1-64367-293-9 (Digital)

Fiction
03.05.19

> "A mind is a terrible thing to waste."
>
> —The motto of the United Negro College Fund

# A NOTE FROM THE AUTHOR

The Take Down is my very first published work of fiction. The Ruiz/Org series will be the first of a series of three. The story was based on greed, money, respect and power, and how at most times, dealing death has a habit of coming back to you. I hope you enjoy and stay tuned for part two coming at the end of 2012 or early 2013.

I would like to first and foremost thank God above for giving me this talent to write for it is something that I love to do. I would like to thank my family for being so supportive of my abilities to see this thing through. To my children, "shine babies, I love you guys to death." And of course the biggest shout out will go to Author Thomas Overton, for seeing the talent and potential in me as well as The Penguin Group, thank you guys. To my family I Love you and let's get these coins!!!!!!

I would appreciate feedback from the readers and fans because it helps a lot to know what you think. You are the backbone of my success.

Drop me a line at: writerayyubi4ever@gmail.com

Stay Blessed!<br>
Lala Ayyubi

# CHAPTER 1

## *1985, Costa Rica....*

In the darkened bedroom, the muffled screams of a woman could be heard on the king sized bed there was a large, naked man who was on his knees. He had the body of an athlete. He was of olive complexion his hair was shoulder length, and jet black. He was leaning over the naked body of the woman. The man, face was poised over the woman's privates, he was about to start sucking her breast, but lifted his head to tell the woman who was screaming for her someone to help her. Your family is dead! I slit your mother's throat, as your father watched." "She's dead!" he told the woman "Bendaho! I killed her and that punk ass father of yours! Now you are mine. Your mother chose Arturro over me and now I'm going to take his most prized possession. Yes, Uncle Darien is going to give you something good." He continued as he leered at her while sticking his finger roughly inside her as he rubbed his hardening dick.

The woman screamed out in pain. "I have to remember this pussy has never been touched. And I will be the one who breaks you in." Darien said.

The woman began to squirm and tried to get away. "There is nothing you can do Maria. I intend to have you regardless of how much you scream and squirm. Your family is dead, so I can do pretty much as I please with you. Come chic, open your legs." He said as he flipped her over on her back.

He forced her legs open and dove down between the woman's legs and began to lick her in her secret place.

"Relax Maria, you will learn to like this and if you're good, I might even let you live."

The woman continued to cry as Darien began to lick on her pussy. One of his large hands held her down while he bent her over the bed. Maria cried out softly, "por favor ya basta. Por favor ya basta." Maria, who was 19 years old, was already a beautiful woman. Her jet black hair hung almost waist length and lay spread underneath her on the bed. Maria was terrified at what was being done and she was scared out of her mind. Darien continued sucking Maria's pussy. He was sticking his fingers in her while licking on her clit. She tried kicking at him crying for Darien to leave her alone, but he was too strong for her. "It's ok. It'll get better for you Maria before long you'll love dick just like all of you whores do." Darien said.

He again began to massage his swollen member maintaining its hardening as he began to push himself inside of her private area.

Maria's screams filled the air as Darien began to move inside her tearing her apart. "Ai, ai this pussy is good. You will learn to love it. Just like your puta mother with her beautiful face and teasing eyes. That bitch said she loved me!" Darien raged as he continued to assault Maria even harder while ranting and raving. "In the end, your father got her and took her away from me. We were raised together. Your father and I, we were like brothers, but we came from very different backgrounds. Your father, Arturro, who at one time was my best friend around about the time my parents were killed, and his family took me in, he was like my blood." Darien uttered as he continued thrusting away on Maria who began to fall in and out of consciousness.

"We did everything together, but once he met Angelina then things changed. We both met her at the same time, but she was more attracted to your father. With his pretty boy looks, his family's money, and ties, as far as Angelina was concerned, I didn't have the family background as he did. She loved the things that money could buy so that counted me out. But during a night of drinking, I tricked your father into signing over all assets and bank accounts to me. I slipped something into his drink to make him sleepy. And since he trusted me completely, he never even looked at what he was signing that night. I told him it was loose ends regarding a business deal we were working on and it would be a piece of cake." Darien said as he humped and grunted inside of her.

"He didn't even check the signatures. Yeah, look at me now. I'm going to be that and finally, Darien Legend, the mother fucking man." he continued as he grunted again and released himself inside Maria. Between her cries, screams, and going in and out of consciousness neither of the two saw or heard the bedroom door slowly open.

After tearing her insides apart, Darien pulled his dick out of her, rubbed her hair, and said, "I think I'm going to hold on to you for a while, but first I'm . . ." he said just as he paused after hearing a click behind his head.

He froze and gradually tried to turn to see who was behind him when a voice said, "Don't move mother fucker! Get your hands off of the girl you sick bastard!" The figure dressed in black held its gun pointed at Darien and then looked towards Maria and said, "Are you able to walk, can you stand?" Feebly, Maria looked toward the figure and then slowly nodded. The figure dressed in black then said. "Go in your room and find something to put on, I'll be there shortly to get you. Undalay, undalay"

Maria lay there for a moment, her body still in shock, but she gradually got up off the bed grabbing the covers off the bed to hide her nakedness. She looked at Darien who had just taken her innocence away forever. Face swollen with tears and her body wrecked with pain, her dark eyes were filled with hate and rage. She spat at him and said. "Morir hijo de puta, burn in hell forever."

"What?" Darien answered not hearing her clearly.

"Die motherfucka!" Maria said to him angrily wrapping the sheet around her body and ran from the room.

The figure in black then turned their attention back to the naked Darien who by this time was lying on the bed. With the gun still pointed as Darien's head, the figure in black held it impatiently and said, "So was your intention to kill off all of the Ruiz family." "Who are you? I can give you riches beyond your wildest dreams." Darien said turning slightly sideways to see who it was covered behind the black bandana.

He was trying to keep the figure talking so that he could reach for his own weapon, but his gun lay on the floor in its holster, along with his clothes.

The figure in black said to Darien, "I'm only going to ask you this one more time. Were your intentions to kill off all of the Ruiz family?"

Darien just shrugged his shoulders.

The figure in black then said "Then where did you put the paperwork that you stole from them?" "What! How do know about that? Who the fuck are you, how do you know so much about me? Do I know you?"

"No, I died a long time ago," The figure in black replied. "Now answer my questions. And tell me what the combination is to your safe under the floor board in your study!"

"Who in the fuck are you?" Darien asked again "and how in the hell do you know so much about me like you know where I keep my important papers and financial records? Is that why your face is covered? You don't want me to know who you are because you know that your life will be over once my people find out about this." Darien said as he tried to lunge for his glock on the floor but he never made it. "I am the bitch that's going to send you to hell mother fucker." The figure said and pointed the semi-automatic weapon at Darien and shot him in the arm that was reaching for his gun. "Uughh, you mother fucker!" Darien yelled. "Wait! Wait!" He screamed at the figure in black who responded by saying, "What's the combination to the safe in your office?"

Darien held his bleeding arm that was shot and pleaded, "Please! I'm fucking rich! I can triple whatever you were paid to do this!"

The figure in black smacked Darien upside his head causing him to scream out in pain and said, "Where's the combination you pedophile fucker?"

"36, to the left, 24 to the right 48 to the left." Darien replied as he cringed in pain.

"Gracias" The figure in black replied and pointed the gun at Darien's exposed penis. Darien started to plead for his life, but the bullets sprayed from the gun rapidly causing him to scream as the bullets ripped his penis to shreds. As Darien cringed in pain, the figure in black raised the gun to Darien's forehead and said, "You can't triple pay back what you've already taken, especially without my permission, Mr. Legend. So take this with you instead on your way to hell." The figure in black pulled the trigger instantly sending Darien to his maker as the bullet ripped thru his skull. As his dead body lay on the bed, the blood from Darien's open mouth and body began to soak the mattress as the figure in black calmly walked away. As the figure walked, it took off the bandana, the black gloves, and dropped them on the floor. The figure un-zipped and untied its black hoodie then reached up and let down a long head of hair. There revealing a woman. She shook her hair out and took off the baggy, black sweat pants, which unveiled her shapely figure that was clothed in designer jeans and a halter top. She then went into the bathroom and got a dry towel. Being extra careful, she wiped the gun clean and dropped it by the body. She walked down the hall to Maria's room, and opened the door. Maria had gotten dressed and was sitting in the corner of the room now fully dressed still in a state of shock, Maria looked up at the woman that stood in the doorway and said "I knew it was you who would save me my sister. Is Darien gone?"

"Si. Un poco, ven conmigo, nadie se daño de Nuevo" Maria's sister Najah stated saying yes, come with me. No one will ever hurt you again. "Come Maria, I am taking you away from here."

Maria got up and walked over to her sister Najahh and asked, "Are mama and papa really dead?"

"si estim ado uno, but their deaths have been avenged and no one will ever touch you again. Come, we have to go now." Najah said.

The little girl turned around and took one last look at her bedroom where she had spent most of her childhood at for the last time. "Adios," she whispered as the two turned and left the room. Najah walked Maria towards the front door of the mansion. Najah knew her younger sister would need medical attention as soon as possible. Psychological evaluation would probably be needed as well. Najah planned on taking her to a private family doctor as soon as she got her little sister to safety. Everything that Maria needed would be provided for her and money would never be a problem for either of them. Her family was the Ruiz family and they were embedded in wealth. Najah half carried her sister to the car and carefully put her into the front seat of a cream colored Mercedes Benz that was parked in the drive way. She buckled her little sister in and told her she would be right back and to be brave until she returned. Najah walked to the trunk of the car and took out a green duffel bag which contained some plastic explosives. She quickly headed back inside the house to lay the explosives that were ready to go. This operation to bring Darien down had been planned for months. Najah looked around the house once more and briefly reminisced of her many memories of her family in this house. Najah snapped out of the happy memories of yesteryear and headed for the safe in the study and she used the combination that Darien had given her. When she heard the safe click Najah twirled the knob on the steel safe door and it opened to reveal a black briefcase. She pulled it out and opened it. Inside were papers and documents that lay on top of stacks of money. Najah put everything inside the briefcase that she carried and closed it. She put the large briefcase by the front door of the mansion and went back and opened a knapsack where she had placed explosives that she quickly put around the house. She placed the last small explosive in the mouth of Darien before quickly going back down stairs and walking to the front door of the mansion. Najah picked up the briefcase, and walked quickly out of the mansion and to the car. Najah put the briefcase in the backseat of the vehicle and then got into the car and looked at her sister and smiled at her as she started it up. She said, "Don't worry Maria, things will be better soon." Najah drove down the long drive way and when they had gotten 2 miles from the house she took out a small device and pushed a red button. A loud boom could be heard in the distance seemingly rocking the land. "What was that noise?" Maria asked. Najah looked at her and said, "The devil paying his dues. The devil paying his fucking dues." The car pushed forward and roared down the road.

# CHAPTER 2

*Harlem, New York ten years later....*

Taj, whose birth name was Tajon walked into the warehouse chewing on a sawak that he got from the Muslim brothers that had the vending tables out in front of the Apollo theatre on 125 Street. He loved chewing on the sticks because they kept his teeth whiter then toothpaste just without the fluoride but with all the natural benefits. Taj began to walk toward the warehouse. He knew he was going to have to change his clothes again before closing shop up for the night. The warehouse was dusty as hell. Taj had on wheat Timberlands with crisp black Sean John jeans and dark polo gear which he knew would pick up the dust quick. He had left his black leather, butter soft trench jacket in the Cadillac Escalade he drove up in. It was getting a little warm being as though it was the month of May, so he was comfortable under the Polo shirt and wife beater he had on. He took his cap off and ran his fingers through his hair. He knew if he hurried up and took care of business, he would have time to go see his barber before meeting up with Najah later on that night. Taj knew she didn't like to be kept waiting, but what she didn't know that he was about

# CHAPTER 3

To get down on one knee and propose to her that night. He loved the shit out of her and he was going to make her officially his. Taj met her through Monet, his boy Sin's wifey. With his dark chocolate skin and whiter than white teeth, Taj had it going on as far as looks go, but he was stone cold when it came to matters of business. At 23, he and his boy Sincere, or Sin as he was called, were millionaires. Young dealer's born from a generation of dealers. The two had known each other from the womb, their fathers were two of the original OG's. Black Ty and Lucifer, part of a click called "The Organization" or "The Org.

Their motto was "Leave no man standing." Lucifer was Taj's father and one of the meanest niggas in Brooklyn, NY at the time. He and Ty had started "The Organization" that followed and strictly enforced the policy of show no mercy. Lucifer's name told tales in the hood. Black Ty's rep was also a force to be reckoned with in the streets. People said "you never saw him coming until it was already too late. Black Ty was said to have killed over 200 men in his time. He taught his son that this game is more than the rep you carry, or the corner you hold. And don't ever let a nigga catch you slipping, a bitch either for that matter. Never let them know your weakness cause another nigga will try to use it against you as well.

# CHAPTER 4

The two men had groomed their sons to take over their lucrative cocaine business and own illegal businesses to wash the money. Their illegal business had grown to a multi-million dollar a year organization. Lucifer told Sin and Taj when they were 13 years old. "Trust no one but each other. Let no one come between the bond and code of this business. One watch the front and one watch the back, and you both watch the workers. Niggas will come at you disguised with the smile of a friend and come back later to slit your throat. There ain't no friend's in this business. Y'all were bought up like brothers. Blood in blood out. And, don't ever get attached to anybody you can't walk away from in 25 seconds flat if the shit hits the fan." Since they were told these words of wisdom, they have strictly abided by that rule.

Taj and Sin were the youngest caked up niggers in Brooklyn. They had no close friends and the associates through the business, were just that, associates of the business. They kept things strict, and their team was tight and on point.

# CHAPTER 5

Therefore there would be nobody to tell tall tales if needed to be dealt with because dead men don't talk. Taj was coming to check the progress of the two new lieutenants he and Sin had just bought on board "The Organization", Rahim and Andre. They were currently on a trial run basis to officially become members of "The Organization." Taj didn't really like the nigga Rahim because something about dude he didn't trust, but the boy came with tight references. Rahim's sister, Ronnie, ran one of their hair salons in the Bronx and she was good peeps so Taj and Sin agreed to give her brother a shot. They both knew from experience that if they gave a nigga an inch and they would take a yard. So that being a good rule of thumb Taj liked to follow, he would still keep an eye on that nigga. Taj wasn't trying to hear about money missing or it getting fucked up. The Organization employed 6 lieutenants that rotated shifts at the warehouse. There were never more than two lieutenants inside at a time in addition to the soldiers that watched and dealt with the day to day shit on the outside. Rahim and Andre were being officially initiated into The Organization that night. Sin and Taj wanted to see what the two were really made of. Once you were in The Organization you were in for life. Although, Taj still had to meet this nigger named Bigz and get two pounds of birds from him at a good price. He still had to drop them off to get seasoned, freeze dried and zip locked in order to hit the market.

# CHAPTER 6

After Taj handled this piece of business, he planned to meet up with his girl Najah for dinner. Bigz was this older cat that had been around when Taj and Sin's dad was still in the game heavy. Bigz was an old school nigger who had a lucrative operation in Long Island and maintained a name that still rang bells a little something out in the streets. Rumor had it that nobody was allowed near Bigz, unless they were already made men, nesting at least 20-30 g's a week out on the streets, minimum. Taj and Sin were not only with Bigz because of their fathers' relationship in the past their names were already out there as making that paper flip to platinum status. Nobody got in with Bigz unless they were getting large paper. The deal with Bigz would be after the meetup with the two new lieutenants, but afterward, he had a special date planned with Najah. Tonight was Taj and Najah's one year anniversary the two had met at Sin's birthday party two years prior.

### .... *two years prior*

When Taj first seen Najah, he was popping bottles of Chriz with his boy Sin in the VIP section of Club Image. Club Image was an upscale club in the Bronx where most upscale hustlers hung out. On this particular night, it was the fall of '97' and Sin's twenty first birthday party. The dance floor was packed and everyone was feeling nice. Taj was just about to raise a toast to his boy Sin when Sin's girl Monet came over to the table with the most beautiful girl Taj had ever seen.

# CHAPTER 7

She had a body to die for and a physique that would lure any man to lose his religion over, lust by far. Long legs, caramel colored skin, and she wore a black, strapless, dress that was cut low in the front ascending her breast. Taj was impressed. Her long hair was pulled up with a diamond clasp. The few loose tendrils that escaped from her upswept hair framed her face making her look good enough to eat. She wore a diamond heart with a big ruby in the center around her neck that rested in between her cleavage. Two carat diamond studs adorned her ears and on her dainty feet she sported black Giuseppe heels with ankle straps. She held a gift in her hand that was firmly wrapped in gold and white wrapping paper with a white bow on top. Her makeup was flawless, un-like most of the chicks in the club who looked as though they were auditioning for a Mabeline commercial. Najah was just naturally beautifully. She smiled as she and Monet walked over to where Taj and Sin were sitting at the VIP table.

"Happy Birthday Sin! So, how old are you now? What all of 21?" Najah teased.

She leaned over to hug, kiss Sin, and hand him his birthday gift. Najah acquired Sin's sizes from Monet earlier in the week so everything she bought him would fit. As Najah leaned over to hug Sin, the sensual smell of her perfume drifted across the table to Taj's nose. "Damn she smelled good" Taj thought to himself as he watched her.

# CHAPTER 8

Sin said, "Thank you baby gurl, but you didn't have to get me anything." Najah laughed and replied, "Well it was hard to buy something for someone who has every thing already," as she tried not to notice Taj, who she had not been formerly introduced to, checking her out.

Sin looked at Taj, smiled, and leaned over toward him and whispered in his ear, "I already see where your little head and big head are going, but let me just put some info in your ear though. Shortie, she good people. She goes to college and she has her own little business as well."

"What are you two whispering about?" Monet asked.

Sin laughed and stood up. He kissed Monet on the cheek and said, "Nothing baby. It's just men talk. Thank you."

He shook the box and said, "ain't no bomb in here is it?"

Najah laughed as she replied, "stop playing boy." She looked Taj deep into his eyes while asking Sin "who is this?"

"My bad, that's my boy Tajan although he prefers being called Taj. Taj, this is Najah." Sin replied.

Taj reached out his hand to kiss hers, "how you doing Najah?" "I'm good," Najah answered as she smiled, "and you?"

"I'm great now that I've seen you," Najah giggled and Taj responded you lit the room up when you walked in. He pointed at the tray of champagne that sat in the center of the table, "Champagne?" he asked. Najah smiled as she looked at the large tray of poured glasses of champagne that sat in the center of the table.

"Ahh, so I see you're a charmer as well as fine." Najah replied as Taj handed her a glass.

## CHAPTER 9

"Open your present baby I want to see what you got." Monet said.

"Damn girl get back. It ain't your birthday," Sin answered back and laughed. He ripped open the box and pulled out a grey cashmere Polo sweater, with matching cap.

"Aww this shit is popping, thanks Najah, good looking'." "Yeah that shit is nice" Monet chimed in.

"Wait, wait, look what I got my baby," Monet said as she reached for her purse. She reached in it and Monet took out a long jewelry box. She gave it to Sin, he opened it, and in it was a man's deluxe, platinum Rolex watch.

Sin looked at it with the eyes of appreciation.

"Damn, thank you baby this is the same watch I was scoping out with you a month ago" Sin said as he leaned over and kissed Monet.

He grabbed her by the hand and they stood up from the table and hugged lovingly. Sin and Monet stopped hugging as she urged Sin to the dance floor.

"Yall should come out here with us." Monet said pulling Sin by the hand onto the dance floor. Taj looked at Najah. "Would you like to dance?"

"Sure." Najah replied to Taj's request.

"I just hope you can keep up with me," Najah said as she got up from the table.

"Ohhh, u got jokes." Taj said and they laughed. "Aight ma let's see what you working with." Taj said as they headed to the dance floor and Biggie" came on.

# CHAPTER 10

The club went crazy causing everybody to get up and hit the floor. They enjoyed each other and danced for a few more songs thereafter. Afterwards, the four of them went back to their tables, talked, and laughed for the rest of the night before finally leaving the club around 5 am. As Taj and Sin waited out front, for their drivers to pull around, Taj turned to Najah and asked "can I get you home safely?" "Mmm, how safe will I be Chocolate?" she replied referring to his handsome dark brown complexion.

Taj smiled, his white teeth flashed briefly and he said, "oh you will be safer than safe ma. Ain't nothing going to touch you in my presence."

"Is that so?" she replied.

"Yep. You can take my word to the bank, baby girl." Taj replied.

"Ok Chocolate, I'll take your word on that". Najah said and turned toward Taj as the cars pulled up in front of them. "Hey girl, Chocolate going see me home . . . . safely." she said smiling as Najah hugged Monet goodnight. "I will hit you in the am." She said "Alright, y'all be good. Monet said as she hugged Najah.

Taj and Sin hugged each other and Taj said, "From the womb to the tomb baby."

"Holla at me in the morning. I gotta talk to you about some shit."

"Alright bro." Sin replied. As he turned toward Monet and said, "come on baby. It's time. Let's go home and start making babies." Monet smiled up at Sin and replied, "you know I got you baby." Her pretty face lit up as the grooves in her dimples deepened as she smiled up at Sin. Monet hugged Taj, and said "take care of my girl, she good peeps. Who knows, yall might even hook up too and get all in love." They all laughed and wished each other a good night. Who would have known? Two years later, Taj and Najah were very much in love and living together.

# CHAPTER 11

## *. . . . present*

The warehouse, also known as the shack was a storage place that the co-owner of "The Organization" Tajon "Taj" Smalls along with Sincere "Sin" Mathers. The two young men at 24 and 25 years old were young millionaires with business ties that stretched out across the five boroughs of New York City. The two had bought the warehouse a couple of years back. It housed retail products for a few local establishments and boxes of money which was cleaned from the drug profits and made look legit. The routine was to clean the money and then it was taken and deposited into a few Swiss offshore accounts. The warehouse was guarded and secured as if it housed the gold stored at Fort Knox. Two strong armed men were posted up in front of the building and surveillance cameras were placed all around the facility. The door to the warehouse was made of solid steel secured with a coded lock. Only Taj and Sin possessed the secret code that could crack the door to gain entrance so when it was time to rotate shifts, Taj or Sin would unlock the door by remote access. They were the only ones who supervised shift changes. There was too much money at various times in the building most men would be tempted so they left no loop holes. As the shifts changed, the soldiers would radio Taj or Sin who would key in the code by remote.

# CHAPTER 12

Four, large rottweiliers roamed the warehouse freely for extra safety measures. The dogs were housed in the building having free rein, trained to, and ready to kill at will any trespassers or unauthorized individuals. As Taj approached the warehouse, he nodded to the man posted in front of the building and gave him dabs.

"What up Nigel, everything cool"?

"Yeah my nigga, shit been pretty quiet. Those two new niggas Rahim and Andre are waiting' for you out back, but I don't trust the boy Rahim." Nigel replied. "Aight, let me go and see where they heads at. I'll get at you" Taj replied as he gave Nigel another dab saying good look and bounced.

He punched in the secret code on the remote watch to open the front door of the warehouse. As Taj opened the steel door, the dogs ran up to him barking because the alarm on the door beeped. After recognizing Taj, they began wagging their tails as he bent to pet them when his cell phone rang. "Hello? . . . . hello? . . . yo, who the fuck is this?" Taj asked. There was an air of silence and no one responded. He looked at the caller i.d, however it read unknown. Prior to this phone call, it was the same result as the other three unknown calls that had occurred during the last week. Someone was calling his cell and saying nothing. Taj hung up the call and called Sin.

# CHAPTER
# 13

"Yo! What's up dog?" He asked as Sin answered the phone. "I hope your slow ass is almost here. You dress slower than my grand mom and she aint got no legs. You know I gotta take care of that thing with the boy Bigz." Sin laughed and said "Yeah my nigga'. I will be there in like 5 minutes." "Traffic was a motherfucker on the crossbronx."

"Aight, I'll meet you at the shack. Them niggas is already at the spot and shit," Taj replied.

"You get the tape?" Sin asked.

"Chill I got you them nigga's going remember this night." Taj replied back.

"Aight my nig . . . I'll see you in a minute." Sin replied.

"One." Taj said as he ended the call.

After checking the warehouse for products that were going out, Taj walked towards the office in the back of the building. He went inside and sat down behind a desk for a minute before heading down into the shack. The shack was where Taj and Sin handled new recruit business for "The Org." Taj stood up and pushed a button revealing a secret door located under a rug that layed in the center of the office. The rug fell down into the hole that formed as the secret door opened. The opening within the floor led down to a cellar area otherwise known as the shack.

# CHAPTER
# 14

Prior to Taj's arrival, the two new recruits, Rahim and Andre had been brought down there blind folded. After the blind folds were removed, they were told to settle in and fall back until further notice. They had been down there for a few days awaiting the arrival of Taj and Sin and supplied with enough food and drink to sustain their wait. No other contact was permitted to the two men because Sin said to leave them there for a couple of days. He wanted to see if the two would show any signs of bitchness or cracking under pressure. What Rahim and Andre didn't know was that in one of the extra rooms of the shack, there was a dude that had been beaten to death a day before after being tortured for hours. Earlier, dude had been placed in a large ice chest to keep his rotting body from stinking up the place. Sin had the body preserved. He needed to make sure the body was dead. That dead body was the result of someone who betrayed the codes of "The Org." As Taj entered the shack, he walked into a small lit room where Rahim and Andre sat at table playing cards. They both looked up as Taj walked into the small room.

"What up freshmen?" Taj said.

He called new hires, recruits until they proved themselves that they could walk and abide by the codes of The Organization." "Y'all up in here chilling, all relaxed and shit." "Yo, what up my nigga?" Andre replied. "We were just waiting for y'all to come through." "Oh yeah, well Sin is right behind me he'll be a sec." Taj replied looking at Rahim, "what up nigga, you alright?" Taj asked.

# CHAPTER
# 15

Rahim and Andre sat at a large wooden desk with a stack of cards resting in the center of it and a spread of cards in each of their hands. The wooden desk took up a good portion of the room as Taj remained standing just inside the entrance way. Taj reached in his pocket and exposed some green that he'd copped earlier in the day. He threw the sack to Andre along with a pack of backwoods to roll it up in.

"Do me a favor kid and roll up something real quick while we're waiting on Sin to get here." Taj asked.

Taj looked at Rahim and said, "you look real familiar to me dog, like I seen you somewhere before? Where you say you from again? Connecticut?"

Taj really knew Rahim was from Washington Heights, an area in the Bronx, however Taj just wanted to see if this time around Rahim would say he was from someplace else.

"He from Connecticut." Andre blurted out. "This some shit you never expected huh?"

"You still want in The Organization nigga?" Taj asked ignoring Andre's bullshit.

"Yeah nigga, I'm good." Rahim replied "Yeah, we good." Andre said.

"Yo nigga, I wasn't talking to you!" Taj shot back. "I was talking to my man right here. Is that going to be a problem for you, speaking out of the blue?" Taj replied. "Yeah, I'm from Connecticut" Rahim chimed in.

"So how long you and . . ." Taj paused, and then said "So how did you say ya'll know each other?"

# CHAPTER
# 16

"I was banging the same chick this nigga was banging until, we bumped heads, when I was leaving her apartment one night." laughed Rahim. "She wasn't about nothing though. There was a lot of niggas hitting that, and I seen the nigger Andre around and knew he was getting a little a paper, so it turned out well for me that we did bump heads at the chick crib"

"Is that right?" Taj responded as he stood up and got a bottle of water from out of the small fridge that was in the store room. "Spark the fuck up what you babysitting for." Taj said to Rahim. The gun holster that was strapped across his back held two glock nines. Burdened with an eerie feeling, he walked back over to the desk as something made him feel real uneasy about this dude Rahim. He put his booted feet up on the table and looked at both of the men.

"So you two nigga's ready for your initiation tonight motherfuckers?" Taj said adjusting his gun holster straps to fit more comfortably. "Tonight, right now, would be the time to turn back before coming on board with The Organization. Cause once you in, its blood in, blood out. There is no leaving this unless its feet up." Taj said staring at both Rahim and Andre in their eyes one by one. "Y'all know this ain't no fucking game! This shit for real, so what's it going to be?"

There was a pause before the two men said anything. After they thought it out and made convincing eye contact with one another, they both replied "We're in." "Alright nigga, we going see" replied Taj. "Now pass me that blunt."

There was noise of someone coming down the stairs. The three men heard the sound of foot steps coming down the steps when Sin appeared. He had a black Burlap bag in his hand that was sagging from the weight that was inside of it.

"Wat up my niggas?" Sin said as he slung the bag to the floor and walked over to Taj and gave him a man hug. "So we ready to rock? Sin asked looking at Rahim and Andre. "So y'all new nigga's ready to do this shit? This organization is a whole new way of life. Your old one is dead, once you in, you in for life." Yo dog . . ." Andre started to say but Rahim cut in looking Sin in the eye. "Well, we give you our lives." There was an air of silence that fell upon the room for a minute before Sin said "Aight, let's do this." He looked at Taj and said, "You ready my nig?"

"Yep" Taj answered and stood up. He looked at Rahim and Andre and said, "come on, we got some unfinished business in the other room."

Taj went to the small chest in the corner of the room and pulled out two black jumpsuits. The material was similar to what raincoats are made out of.

"Put these on." Taj said to the two recruits. Sin picked up the bag from the floor, and turned towards the door. "I'll be upstairs" he said as he walked back up the steps, back into the office, I got something to handle real quick." Taj turned to the two recruits and said, "Follow me, oh and make sure you bring them rubber gloves with you." Taj and the two recruits walked down a small corridor and stopped in front of a closed door. Taj opened the door to a small, dimly, lite, dark room, walked into the room with the other three men behind him. The room was a storage place for crates of hair product that held cans of a special kind of non-detectable, plastic hair spray cans that were filed with large amounts of cocaine, that was discreetly ship to various parts across the city, disguised as hair spray. In one corner of the room there was a metal chair with a man tied to it and his head hung low. His battered face spilled blood forming a small puddle underneath the chair. The man's white wife beater was dirty and coated with blood which spilled from the gashes on his face.

# CHAPTER 17

Taj walked over to the unconscious man, and kicked him.

"Wake up nigga! This is your life calling you!" Taj said as he kicked the chair a second time. The man woke up and moaning and groaning. He began to whine and beg for his life. "Please man, it wasn't me!" He cried out.

"Shut your bitch ass the fuck up! We got your shit on tape, we gave your stinking ass a chance to make some money and you going to steal from us? We gave you just enough rope to hang your ass, and you did and bite the hands that feed you, nigga?" Taj barked.

# CHAPTER 18

Taj turned back towards the two men. "Yo my nig . . . bring that bag" he said to Rahim, when the bag was handed to Taj, he pulled out a short gage saw and gave it to Rahim. "It's show time." He said. Taj then pulled out a large machete and gave it to Andre. "See that nigga right there, he was a runner for us, and a motherfucker got greedy. So now ya'll rookie nigga's is about to be schooled on what happens to nigga's who steal from The Organization. Andre looked at Rahim, who looked at Taj, but said nothing. Taj pulled a large bowie knife from his boot he bent over the screaming man tied to the chair. "Let me help you out dog" Taj reached inside the man's mouth and gripped his tongue and with one slice, cut it off. Blood started squirting from the man's mouth as his body started to thrash in the chair.

# CHAPTER
# 19

His moans become louder, as the blood poured out of his mouth and down the front of his shirt. Taj stood up, the bloody knife he had just used in his hand and turned to Andre and Rahim and said. "Initiation part two new niggas, as the moaning man in the chair began thrashing around in the chair. Taj turned back towards the thrashing man and said "Damn nigga you still refuse to shut the fuck up? Matter of fact, how about this when you get to hell nigga tell em Taj sent you." as he sliced the man's throat. The man in the chair thrashed around violently in the chair before taking his last breath. Taj wiped the blade again on the dead man's shirt and put it back in the sheath that was tucked in his boot. He turned again to Rahim and Andre. "Rookies, I want you two niggas to cut this mother fucker up into pieces, leave the head separate from the body and cut off the hands. There is a can of acid over there in corner, pour it on the fingertips, so the prints can't be identifiable and then pour some in the mouth of his head so that all the teeth are covered with that shit.

# CHAPTER 20

We want no identifiable dental records that could come back and be traced to "The Org. We are going to bury the head and hands separately the body parts will be dumped in the river over in Spanish Harlem." Taj walked across the room and reached into the closet and pulled out a large box of black contractor bags and threw it down on the floor next to the dead man in the chair when the body is cut up, bind everything in garbage bags and tape them up tight. It's tape in the bag next to the acid. Wrap each bag with heavy chains to weigh the bags down." Taj looked at his watch and said "I'll be back down in an hour y'all should be done by then. After you finish hose down the basement floor, making sure all the blood was rinsed down the drain take these bags outside and put them in the grey pickup truck parked out back. We are going to use the pickup to dispose of the parts down along 127th and Riverside over near Spanish Harlem.

# CHAPTER 21

Down by the docks where those warehouses are, at night its dark and quiet once business is done for the night.

"Make sure no nosey mother fuckers around, use that wheel barrow over there to put the bags in so you can roll them to the van and load it up." Make sure you lock the doors and come back here and report back to me." Taj said You got it?" Taj asked the two men. "Yeah we got it replied the two recruiters." "Then let's get to work" Taj said and walked out the room leaving the two men to start the business at hand. Taj walked back into the office where Sin was sitting behind the desk, going over the journal book where they kept records of the functioning of the business. They only kept paper records for the legal businesses they owned, all illegal transaction were kept on the mental between the two of them. "So, what's up, what you think about these new nigga's Sin?" Taj asked him. Sin looked up at him and took the tooth pick he had in his mouth, "I don't know yet, I can't put my finger on it, but that nigga Rahim just don't fucking seat right with me. I could swear I seen that nigga before, so you know that shit going bug me until I remember where I've seen him before. In the meantime, we going keep a real close eye the two of them, but Rahim for sure.

# CHAPTER 22

"If I remember where I've seen him and it was on some foul shit, that get two the dome plain and simple, you already know how we do it?" Sin said. Taj rolled up a blunt and lit it and said so when these niggas are done, I gotta roll my nigga, I got some shit to do before meeting up with Najah at the crib later, it's our one year anniversary, I'm proposing to baby girl tonight." Taj said as he pulled out a ring box and opened it to reveal a 4.5 carat heart shaped diamond engagement ring. "Damn!! Now that's what's up" Sin said getting up to give Taj some love as they man hugged. "Now you know Monet is going be all on my ass now that Najah got a ring, I ain't going never hear the end of this shit." Sin said as the both of them laughed. Taj put the ring box back in his pocket and handed Sin the blunt. "So how are things looking on the books?" Taj asked. "Everything is adding up as it should be now this nigga is dead, Sin responded. "And that's just on the legitimate side, I was about to go over the drops next." He said as he passed the blunt back to Taj. Before Sin could continue what he was going to say next Rahim and Andre came back in from the outside. "It's done" Rahim said looking at Sin and Taj "Aight lets do this and get this shit over, that was fast, yall nigga's must have a knack for this shit. Taj said standing up and looking at his watch, before looking at Andre and Rahim. "That knack could come in real handy at times. We ready?" Taj asked Sin. "Yeah, I'll ride with these niggas and we can drop the truck back here after we handle this business." Sin responded.

# CHAPTER 23

"I know you got that thing to handle that piece of business we discussed earlier, so go ahead and meet up with Bigz and go handle that, I got this." Sin said to Taj. "Aight my nigga, I'm out" Taj said as he and Sin dapped hands and the four men separated to go about their agenda's for the night.

Out of town, Najah and Monet were shopping at the gallery mall in Philadelphia, Pa. The two of them had drove out to Philly to meet one of the sorority sisters from college for lunch and then do some shopping. Her name was Jazzmin, although she preferred to be called Jazz. Jaz was a very pretty girl, she was from Baltimore. Her father, an Italian immigrant who owned several shipping company's across the metro areas of New York, Philadelphia, Delaware and Baltimore. Jazz's mother, Marie, was black but from a good family, who maintained residency back in Queens, NY. Marie was a pediatrician who owned her own practice in a ritzy part of Bensonhertz, Brooklyn.

# CHAPTER 24

In the looks department, Jazz got a mixture of her Italian's father dark curly hair, and his dark brown eyes, her honey complexion she took from her mother as well as her curvy body. Jazz was now the couple's only child, after her brother Antonio was killed by a drunken driver when he was 17. The three young women had not seen each other since their graduation from college three years prior. The three women strolled down the floors of the galleria mall playing catch up. The three talked often, but it was rare they were all able to get together in one city. "So Jazz Najah said to her, what have you been up to?" "Well right now I'm just getting ready to go into med school in a couple of months, so I have been doing a lot of studying and preparing myself for that. My parents are really on my back about keeping my grades up, I think my dad will have a coronary if I didn't become a doctor, especially after all the tuition he has paid and will still be paying for at least another 3 years until I can began my internship at a hospital." Jazz responded. "Damn girl med school, Dr. Jazzmin Santegelo, I love it" joked Najah. "That's what's up we all doing the damn thing, can life get any better?"

# CHAPTER 25

Monet asked as the three young women slapped each other high fives "Yeah that's what's up so you and Brian still doing that long distance thing?" Monet asked Jazz. "Yeah, for the moment we will see how that goes. Shit I have a hard enough time with him and his bullshit when I'm home, so long distance going to be a fucking trip!! Jazz laughed "Maybe he'll fly right, after 3 years together he better, my daddy is Italian, I don't to want to have to get him to put a hit on his ass." Jazz laughed. "You stupid" laughed Monet, but I know that's right, the girls laughed as they continued to browse the mall, when, Najah's phone rang, she looked at the caller id, and stared at it for a moment with a slight frown on her face.

# CHAPTER
# 26

"What's the matter girl?" asked Monet, "what's up" Najah looked up from the phone at Monet "It's my grandmother calling from Costa Rica." Listen you guys go ahead, I'll catch up in a minute." Najah said to the two women. "Are you sure Naa?' Monet asked her. "Yeah girl go ahead, I'll catch up, to you in a minute." Najah responded. "Alright Monet said, we will be down at the Gucci store as she and Jazz walked away. Najah watched them walk away, before she pressed the 'missed call" option to return the call. She held the phone up to her ear, as the voice on the other end spoke softly to her. "So Najah your sister said you were coming home for a visit? You are bringing guest with you, is that right?" Najah's grandmother asked from the other end of the phone, "Si Abuela (yes grandmother) but we are not going to be there until Friday evening instead of Friday morning." Najah responded. "Nieta querido (dear granddaughter) "Abuela English, please"

# CHAPTER 27

Najah interrupted her grandmother before she continued anymore in Spanish. Najah's grandmother, Isabella was born and raised in a little city right outside of Costa Rico she grew up speaking and hearing Spanish around her all the time. When she married Najah's Grandfather, Antonio he helped groomed her into the ways and culture of the outside world of Costa Rica. "Meha your grandfather wants to see you as soon as you and your guest arrive. He said to tell you It's important, but that's all the information I could get out of him as to what is so important." Isabella said. "Did he say what it is about? "Najah asked. "No, he said to make sure that you try to make seeing him at his office the first stop you make when you get here.

## CHAPTER 28

"Najah, he said it was something to do with Darien." Isabella said. Najah almost dropped the phone, as the memories from ten years ago came flooding back from that night. Najah was quiet so long her grandmother asked her over the phone. "Meha are you ok?

# CHAPTER 29

The term "Meha" which means my dear in Spanish made Najah think of when she were a little girl and she would visit her grandparents sometimes for the summer and for a brief moment she missed those times when her parents were still alive. "Yes Abuela I am fine, listen, tell buelo I will see you guys soon, I get in Friday evening at 6pm. I sent you guys the itinerary in your emails so you guys will know what time to meet us at the airport." Ok, I have not been online today, but I will get on it later." Najah's grandmother responded "You have been away from home to long Najah and we can't wait to see you, I love you." "You too Abuela" Najah responded back, as they hung up the phone.

# CHAPTER
# 30

Najah sank down onto one of the little lounge seat's that were scattered throughout the mall for people to sit down on. Najah's mind went back to ten years ago when her parents were killed. Najah and her younger sister Maria went to live with her grandparents it was safer for them to be closer to family. The Ruiz family owned mostly all of the small islands in Costa Rico. Najah grandfather, Enrique had started the family business in the very lucrative drug trade. From there he and his soldiers had expanded the family business to Corporate offices and several small chains of storefront properties. Enrique had two sons and Najah's mother Maria who was the apple of his eye. When Maria had met Arturro and married him with her father's permission. Enrique had built them a beautiful 10 bedroom mansion on one of the smaller islands. Although, Maria was Enrique's only daughter, she was trained to fight and use a weapon along with her brothers as children. All three were all as deadly as professional assassins. So it was only natural that when Najah and her sister came to live with their grandparents, they were trained to protect themselves fully capable to kill at will. The night of her parent's murder a very good friend of the family whose name was Darien had drugged Arturo and Maria's wine after the three had spent a night together out together at charity benefit. Najah was over at a classmates house spending the night, but little Maria had been at home with the nanny. Najah had felt ill at her friend's and decided to come back home, it was she who had discovered her parents mutilated bodies, and found Uncle Darien raping her little sister. Najah had made sure he would never breathe again. Maria now 21 years old, 8 years younger than Najah still lived on the island with their grandparents and was now a stunning woman. All of their parent's assets and joint properties were split between the two girls so they were both very well off. When Darien thought he had their parents sign papers to secretly get their money, were null and void if their parents were murdered instead of dying of natural causes. So Darien's intention to stage Najah's parent's death as a burglary gone bad would have been for nothing, he would not have gotten a dime of their money. Since that night, the two sisters were inseparable, and they never

spoke about that night, not one word. Antonio Enrique, their grandfather and his sons had come after getting a call from Najah and disposed of Darien's body. That night was never to be mentioned again.

# CHAPTER 31

All these years later, that night was never mentioned again, so Najah wondered what was behind the message her grandfather had sent. "Najah?" she came back to present to see Monet standing there. "Girl what's up, everything ok with the fam?" Monet asked. "Yeah, my grandparents are just getting old that's all" they worry about me sometimes." Najah replied. She had never given to many family details to Monet, preferring to keep her family business, family business for the time being. She had never even given Taj info on her family, just telling him they owned some business in Costa Rica, but not the magnitude of how much the Ruiz family actually controlled. Which included most of the surrounding islands in Costa Rica and several controlling business interest in New York, Chicago and New Jersey.

# CHAPTER 32

"My family can't wait for us to get down there especially since I have not been home in two years." Najah said. "Oh, girl I can't wait to get down there either, just to get a break." Monet responded. "Oh and Jazz went to buy those Manola boots from Macy's and then we can start heading back to the city. Hopefully we can beat some of that turnpike traffic going back." Monet stopped speaking as Jazz walked up on them, "Hey ladies, yall ready to blow this place?" "Yeah we gotta get back, tonight is me and my baby's one year anniversary and I got something freaky for my boo tonight." smirked Najah Yeah, I bet your little hot ass does, laughed Monet. "I don't see nothing wrong, with a little bump and grind" Monet sang the lyrics from an R Kelly song. "Aint nothing wrong with being a freak for your man girl." said Jazz, "Because what you won't do . . . . some other freak will" they all chorused and laughed.

# CHAPTER
# 33

They hugged and kissed and promised to meet up again soon, and they departed ways. On the way back to New York, Monet was driving behind the wheel of her Lexus coupe. The cd system played the low sounds of Mary J Blige's hit "What's the 411" "So what your little nasty self got planned for Taj tonight?" Monet. Najah smiled well first we got tickets to see Mary J at the coliseum, after the show, I got the boy Derick shutting down his soul food restaurant for us for a couple of hours, and he will have it hooked up for us a little romantic dinner and then once we get back to the house, and I got the Jacuzzi all set up with candles and music, and well you know." Najah paused and smiled. "Break him off a little something, something" Laughed Monet. "And you know this . . . . man" Najah said. They smacked hands.

## CHAPTER 34

Taj and Sin had parted an hour earlier in the evening. Taj was on his way to get a shape up and beard trim before going home to get dressed. He had already met with Bigz and Taj had already had his people pick up the work and get it ready to hit the streets. His phone vibrated, the called id came up as an unknown number. "Who the fuck is this" he thought, he ignored the call. A few minutes later it vibrated again, same thing unknown number, now this shit was starting to piss him off. "Yo, who the fuck is this playing on my phone" he thought again. It was crazy because Taj changed his phone numbers frequently to keep the trace effect off his phone calls, and only a select few had the number. He rejected it again. He pulled up in front of the barber shop, he looked in the rearview mirror as his security parked behind him as well one parked across the street. He opened the door to the shop as two of the security walked in with him. "I'm in and out" Taj said to them as his phone vibrated again.

# CHAPTER
# 35

He looked at the id, unknown again this time he answered, "Speak" he said into the receiver as he sat down in the barber chair. "So why haven't you been returning my calls Taj?" Yo, who is this?" Oh so you don't know me now, you wasn't saying that shit when you was in my pussy, now was you?" Yo! Asia, I told you stop calling my phone, I am with my girl now for real, and I already told you once, me and you weren't ever going to go nowhere beyond sex and the cheese I threw you, hold your position Asia, you knew what it was and now you want to catch feelings and shit? I am not trying to hear that, you did for me and I did for you, end of story, period." Taj spoke harshly into even the phone. "Taj I am pregnant" the voice on the other end said. "What! Yo look I am the barber shop getting a haircut I'm going to hit you back when I get out of here, I can't talk about this shit right now" he said and clicked the phone off. "Damn! Taj said as he sat down in the chair. Everything alright dog, Keith the barber asked. "Yeah son just got to take care of some shit." Taj responded back. By the way, what's up with that kid from 127th street, does he still have that storefront up there for sale?" Taj asked Keith. "Yeah and as a matter of fact, I seen the nigga earlier today and he said for you to get at him." Keith said. Aight I'm going to do that." said Taj, his phone vibrated again it was Najah so he picked it up. "Hey baby, what's up, nothing what you doing?" I am taking a bubble bath getting ready for tonight." Najah replied, I just called to tell you I love and please don't be late baby" she said. "Nah I got you, and I will not be late." Taj replied, I am going to be on time ma, I know how special tonight is going to be. This is our night and I'll be there on time." Taj responded.

# CHAPTER
# 36

"Alright baby I will see you later, be careful and I love you baby." Najah said as she hung up the phone. "As I was saying" Taj said to Keith, "I will get at dude later on. I am out but I'll see you next week, same time." Taj said as he and the barber exchanged love hugs. Then Taj and his security detail left the shop, and disappeared into the night.

Meanwhile back at Taj's and Najah's house, Najah had gotten out of the bath tub and put on her silk robe that was hanging on a hook on the back of the bathroom door. She pulled her hair loose from the rubber band that was holding it up while she took her bath. Najah walked into the large bedroom, the plush carpet cushioned her feet as she walked towards a large king size canopied bed that occupied a large area of the room. There were white and gold drapes that covered the large, bay windows, which matched the spread that covered a large, king sized bed.

# CHAPTER
# 37

A portrait of Taj and Najah hung over the bed, which had been painted by an artist friend of Taj's. There was a large screened television that hung over the fire place in the room. Two large walk in closets, which one was opened already with the light on inside. As Najah sat down at the vanity table and began to blow dry her hair, she noticed a blinking red light on the alarm panel. "Security breach" Najah said to herself. She pushed a small button on the panel and several small screens appeared next to the alarm display. They gave views of the entire house and property, as she viewed of the grounds outside, she did not see any of the security detail out front, she quickly panned to the inside of the house, as she switched from the viewing the family room to the kitchen, she caught a dark movement in the camera and she panned back to the family room.

# CHAPTER 38

As she did she noticed 3 masked figures, dressed all in black. Her heart racing Najah quickly got up and went over to the walk in closet, she clicked a button inside the closet and the row of clothes hanging up slid to the side to reveal a wall of weapons, bullets, spare cell phones and rechargeable cell and computer batteries and a small safe. Inside the safe she knew was about 25, 000 dollars in cash. Taj called this room the panic room. Surveillance cameras were placed in this room as well. Along the wall, there was stocked canned goods and water, if need be they could hold up inside the panic room for weeks. Najah picked up two 9 mm's and slid the clips in. She bound her hair back up and quickly threw on a jump suit that was hanging in the closet. She darted back into the bedroom looking at the video surveillance camera and noticed the men were getting closer to the stairway to come up stairs. She put one of the 9's in her waistband and picked up her cell phone.

# CHAPTER 39

Najah called Taj's phone, as she cut off the lights in the bedroom and crept towards the door. "Baby, come home right away, somebody's in the house" Najah whispered. "What! Who is in the house, baby what's going on?" Taj said into the phone. "I don't know Taj, but I do not see the security detail anywhere. Najah said as she crept toward the bedroom door and crept down the hallway. "Baby just get here, I gotta go, they might hear me, ok, please hurry" She hung up. "Wait! Naaa baby?" Fuck! Fuck!" Taj tried calling her back, but got no answer. Fuck! Exclaimed again out loud as he speed up faster, his security detail right on his tail. He called a number on his phone, "Yo! Something is going down at my crib, get a few of the niggas and meet me at the crib Sin. If something happens to Najah, I'm not even going to think about that shit Sin. I'm almost to the house, just get there ok I'm getting ready to try Naa again she called that one time and now I can't get any answer. I will be at the house in five minutes." Taj said. "Nigga, I'm already on the way, and I got the security detail with me. We will be there in ten minutes." Sin responded.

# CHAPTER 40

"But what's up with those security detail niggas for the house?" Sin said to Taj.

"Najah said she aint fucking see them no where on the surveillance cameras and none of them niggas are answering their cell phones." Taj said into the phone. "If something happens to Najah dog, somebody going die tonight."

"You better believe it." Sin responded back.

Back at the house Najah had crept down the hall, she could hear faint sounds below she looked over the banister of the darkened stairway. She could see one figure coming slowly up the stairs that led to the second floor. She laid down flat on her stomach on the floor, there was a large rubber plant next to the stairs that she used to shield her body in the darkened hallway and waited until she could see the top of the man's head as he crept up the steps.

# CHAPTER 41

As he got to the landing at the top of the steps, Najah swung from behind the plant and shot the man once in the mouth, once in the face. Bong! Bong! The man fell backwards back down the stairs, his soul immediately exiting his bloodied body. She heard running footsteps on the floor beneath her. Najah sat on top of the railing banister, her strong legs gripping either side and she leaned her body backwards on the railing so that she was hanging so that she could see the other two men as they climbed the stairs and hit them both at once. The way the hallway was situated, it was too dark to really see Najah in her black track suit, so she had the advantage on the two. As the first man came up the stairs slowly, he stepped over the fallen body of the first man Najah had shot. As he leaned against the wall to slide his way up the stairs, Najah aimed slowly, he looked up at the last minute, as she shot twice to each of his eyes. Bong! Bong!

# CHAPTER 42

Najah hoisted herself back up on the railing and jumped down behind the large rubber plant breathing heavily. The third man came running up the stairs he had an Uzi that was spraying bullets all over the staircase and hallway. Najah ran down the hall, back to her bedroom, she ran inside the panic room and shut the heavy iron door and locked it from the other side. Rata tat! tat! tat! tat she could hear the Uzi spraying bullets coming closer to the bedroom. She could hear the man still shooting in the darkened hallway outside the bedroom. She sat still in the room and took out her cell phone and text Taj, "baby I am cornered in the panic room. I got two of them.

# CHAPTER 43

"There is one more with an Uzi." She did not want to risk the shooter hearing her talk on the phone. Although the panic room would be hard to find, there was an automatic switch on the inside of the room that was activated as soon as she bolted herself inside that would close the outside door and move the clothes in the closet back into place. She heard a crash downstairs, the sound of many running feet coming up the stairs and all she heard was shooting for a couple of minutes. She then heard Taj screaming her name. "Najah!! Baby!! where are you?" He screamed out. She looked at the cameras and all she saw was Taj and Sin and several men that where with them. Najah called Taj's phone. "Baby I am alright, I am in the panic room." She said "I'm coming, before she could get the words out her mouth, she heard the outer door open to the panic room and then the second door opened up. Najah leaped in Taj's arms as he hugged her to his body and swung her around before putting her back down and looking her all over.

# CHAPTER 44

"Baby are you alright, did they hurt you?" Taj asked. Sin was standing right behind him with several armed men he smiled at Najah and Taj and said "Damn! Baby sis, I'm glad to see you, damn I'm glad to see you ok." Sin said as he hugged her as well. Najah was shaking as he held her. "I am ok big brother" she replied. "Damn baby I do not know what the fuck I would have done if something had happened to you." Taj said. "Excuse me boss man" Taj turned his head back towards the bedroom door. The head of his security detail, Abdul was standing in the doorway of the bedroom.

# CHAPTER 45

Abdul was in the Special Armed forces for 6 years as a special agent, expertly trained on how to kill, before leaving the unit and began to work for himself. "Yes?" Taj responded. "The perimeter has been secured sir, and the other security detail has been found" well some parts of them. He stopped and looked at Najah "Ms Najah, I'm so glad your okay." Abdul said to her. Then Abdul looked at Sin and the three armed security detail that all stood in the bedroom as well. "May I talk to you in private?" Abdul asked Taj. "Yeah, give me a minute, go down stairs, make sure them niggas got two cars at the front gate and I'll be down in a minute." Taj responded. Taj looked back at Najah kissed her and said "baby I'm so sorry about our special night being ruined but we going make this night up baby, I promise. But in the meantime I'm going need you to quickly pack a bag for you and one for me, pack at least for a couple of days. We can get whatever else we need later once we get settled some place temporarily."

# CHAPTER
# 46

Sin had pulled the security detail in the corner while Taj and Najah talked quietly. Najah looked around their bedroom there were bullet holes all in the walls and blood splattered on the door of the bedroom and piece of what looked like brain matter. The vanity mirrors in the master bedroom had been shattered by the spray of bullets, as the third one lies. "Yes, I think this house has pretty much had it." Najah said to Taj. "Baby listen forget this house, we can buy 5 more just like it." Taj said "We are going to stay at a suite for a little bit til things cool off. I going to have my nigga Doc, get us some property real quick first thing in the am. We've been infiltrated baby, I'm not sure by whom, but I will before sun down tomorrow, believe that. Did they say anything to you?" Taj asked. "No baby, I was getting ready to get dressed for tonight and I saw the alarm light blinking, so I got the guns out and called you." Najah said. "Damn! Taj exclaimed "Who the fuck were those niggas, they were professional, they had to be, to get past the security detail." Taj said.

"And these niggas wasn't black my nigga, they looked almost Cuban or Spanish." Sin said from the other side of the room where he stood with the body guards.

"Span… Spanish?" Najah stuttered biting her lip, she never saw the gun men's faces being that they wore ski mask. Taj looked at Najah and said baby, were gonna leave these two men up here while you pack and I need to find out what the fuck this is about. "These mother fuckers came in my house! Nobody comes here but Sin and Monet, and the security detail" Taj said, he looked at his baby listen hurry up ok, we have to go, for me just pack the usual shit, as far as my gear." "I'll have the housekeeper come in and clean this shit and get ready to sell it. Baby damn, I'm so glad nothing happened to you, but the looks of it, I see you held your own baby girl."

# CHAPTER 47

"Taj said and gave Najah a smile both them niggas on the stairs got holes in their domes. It looks like those shooting lessons you and Monet took a couple of months ago really paid off." He said. Taj had no idea that Najah was trained as well as any elite soldier in the ways of killing. There was some scuffling noise down stairs, the surveillance monitors in the bedroom had been shot out by stray bullets. Taj and Sin looked at each, other as the security detail put their hands on their weapons that were placed discreetly under their jackets. Before they could move, Abdul's booming voice could be heard saying that everything was ok. Taj turned back to Najah and gave her another kiss, and said. "Baby, I will be right down stairs talking to these niggas, call me when you're ready for the men to bring the bags down. He turned to walk towards the bedroom door, and paused and turned around, "So Naa, you really shot those two dudes huh?" "Yeah baby, Najah replied, I guess I got lucky."

# CHAPTER 48

"I'm proud of you baby, you held It down tonight" Taj said as he walked out the door with Sin and back down the stairs. Two men stood outside the room on either side of the doorway. Najah walked to the closet quickly, she got out her luggage case out. She took down a small shoe carry case from the shelf as well. She quickly filled the suitcase with a couple pair of designer jeans, some shirts. She walked back into the bedroom from the walk in closet. Najah stepped over broken glass that had shattered from the vanity mirrors to one of the large highly polished wooden dressers that stood in the corner of the room. She threw in some undies and a few things to sleep in. Najah walked over to Taj's large walk in closet and got his large leather Louis Vuitton luggage satchel and begin to put some things together for Taj. Najah reloaded both 9's from the wall artillery and put them her in cases. She also put a small 22 in her purse. She put her kicks on and threw some personals and toiletries in a smaller bag and put them over by the bedroom door. Najah went back into the panic room and she dialed the combination to the safe, but before she opened it, Najah walked back out into the bedroom, and asked the security detail to come in and get the bags.

# CHAPTER
# 49

Once they had gotten both her and Taj's bag and taken then to the top of the stairs for some of the men below to come up and get. Najah then went back inside the panic room with a large Louis Vuitton book bag which she filled quickly with the money that was in the safe. She knew Taj would want her to bring it. Before going down stairs, she had one more call to make, she opened her cell phone and dialed a number . . . "Hola abuela, puedo hablar con el abuelo?" Hello grandmother, may I speak to grandfather? Najah said in a low voice.

Downstairs Taj was talking to the men, Abdul was talking in a low tone, boss we found all three of the security detail, but we couldn't tell who was who because their heads were separated from the bodies and missing." Abdul stated. "Whoever did this, got in without tripping the first alarm, but good thing you had the second alarm installed a couple of weeks ago that sent the alert to the police, but I told my peoples over there that would handle the situation. Also the men that Ms Najah killed were from as far as I could tell from outside of the country, like Columbia, Cuba, some place like that. One of them had a Cuban cigar that I have found located only in areas along those regions. Also, they sported dragon tattoos with the seal of old Spanish money on it. I took pictures and sent a picture of the tats to an ex military buddy of mines.

# CHAPTER
# 50

He used to be stationed out there in that territory and knows all the local guerilla and terrorist activist in that area well. Since it's so late, he may not get a chance to find out much until the am, if he can't tell us who they belong too." Abdul stated. "Ok, but I want you on this Abdul, you hear me, whoever did this I want them found." Taj said. But do not kill them when you find them, ya'll can torture them all you want until I get there but keep them alive." He said. "Don't worry boss, I am all over it." Abdul replied. He turned towards his crew and began speaking quietly to the men to give them instructions. Taj, vibrated again, he looked at the id again, unknown, fucking Asia would call at a time like this he thought to himself, he ignored the call and turned to Sin and said "we are about to be out of here." As two security detail came down with Taj and Najah's bags. Taj turned back to Sin and said,

# CHAPTER 51

I'm going to run up and get Naa and we are out!! Taj ran up the stairs and told the two men posted by the bedroom to go and wait by the stairs. He went in and Najah was putting a baseball cup over her dark hair that been pushed up into a neat bun. "Baby you ok?" He asked Najah. "Don't worry this shit is not going to spoil our anniversary I still got a surprise for my baby. We are going to check into that chateau that we stayed at out when we bought this place and it was being finished after we bought it and added additions?" Taj put her down as Najah replied yes and gave him the bag of money. They walked to the door of the bedroom and towards the stairs. "Hold up baby" Taj said to Najah as Taj told the two security detail to come with them in his car he would add one more man in the corner from the group of men downstairs. His arm around Najah they walked down the stairs into the large foyer where Sin and the rest of the men were waiting ready to go. Taj whispered in Najah's ear.

# CHAPTER
## 52

"We are going have the whole floor this time, so you can have your choice of suites or we can have our anniversary night in each and every one of them." Taj smiled at her as they got the front door kissed her. They walked out the front door, Abdul was standing out front, there were men posted by the waiting vehicles. Sin said to Taj so were going to follow behind you, the other two cars will follow behind us." "Alright, let's do this." Taj responded as he and Najah got into a black escalade. Abdul closed the door after them and jumped in the front driver's seat. They drove in silence for a bit, before Taj took Najah's hand, "So what you got up your sleeve for tonight?" he asked. Najah smiled and said "it's a surprise, and if I tell you it won't be one now will it?" She smirked "Yeah alright smart ass." Taj laughed, his phone vibrated again. He took it out and looked at the caller id, "unknown" again. "I think its time to change this number again" he said. "I keep getting these non id calls. Abdul in the morning call dude and tell him to get me a new number please." "I got it boss man." Abdul replied looking in the rearview mirror checking the detail behind and for anyone following them.

# CHAPTER

# 53

As they pulled up into the front of the Marriot Suites, Abdul got out and opened the door for Najah, the other security detail walked over to them and the four of them went inside to check them in. The adjourning suites next to theirs were left empty except for two of them which would house the security detail. Sin and Taj spoke briefly in the front lobby Najah had been taken up stairs to the rooms. Sin was getting ready to go home to Monet and bring her back to the hotel she wanted to be close to Najah in reference to the chain of events that had taken place that night. He and Taj gave each other man hugs rooms Taj told Abdul that he and Najah would be rolling out within an hour they were going out for the night. Taj also told Abdul to make sure all security was on point and posted by all exit doors and the parking lot entries as they rode the elevator to the top floor. Although Taj knew Abdul knew his job and knew it well, when it came to their lives, he wouldn't second guess anything.

    Rahim and Andre were across town at the strip club they were drinking and sitting at one of the tables that were in front of the stage. There was a stripper there named Tasty, she was slowly sliding down the pole on stage her apple shaped bottom was shaking to the beat of "Ride it" by Ginuwine. As she got to the floor she slowly turned around and her 38 b's stood at attention and she slowly walked to the edge of the stage. Her pussy hair was trimmed into the shape of a heart. She was sucking on a cherry blow pop, and she got down on her knees in front of Rahim and Andre, looking them in the eyes she took the lollipop out of her mouth and stuck it in her pussy slowly as she licked her lips. Rahim and Andre both watched as well as every man in the club.

# CHAPTER
# 54

As Tasty took out the lollipop Tasty pointed it toward them smiling and mouthed "want to taste it?" Andre stood up shouting "Yeah baby!! And he threw some money up on stage at her. "You better stop tricking your money on these hoes nigga." Rahim laughed Andre, just laughed and said "whatever nigga" and walked over to the stage, since Tasty was naked except the garter belt on her thigh, so he tucked $50.00 into it. The security mean mugged Andre until he sat back down in the chair and continued to watch Tasty put on her set. Tasty sashayed back to the center of the stage and continued her show. Andre was mesmerized Rahim just sat laughing at him. "Nigga you are crazy as hell, fucking with these hoes."

# CHAPTER
# 55

"Whatever nigga, but check it.... look over there. Ain't that the dude over there that robbed and raped your sister a little while back?" Andre asked, Rahim looked through the darkened room until he spotted the dude that Andre had pointed out. "Yeah that's that nigga Josh." Andre said, "Oh this nigga up in here tricking the money he stole from my sister." He thought he got away with that shit, until the lady across the hall described this nigga to a tee." Stupid ass nigga took off his mask as he was coming out my sister's apartment." Andre stood up from the table, "Yo, let's wait outside for this nigga man." It's too many people up in here right now" Andre said. Rahim stood up, "let's do this playa" Rahim looked over again at the table that Josh was sitting at, and quickly looked away. He only got one dude with him, and there is more than 10 empty bottles on the table between." "So these niggas drunk too, so you know they ain't on point like they should be." Raj said, the two men walked outside, and opened the door to Andre's Lincoln Navigator, and got in.

# CHAPTER
# 56

They pulled down the street where the street lights were not as bright and made a u-turn and then parked the car so that they could face the crowd coming out at closing time. "The strip joint close in a half hour" said Rahim. "So we will wait til everybody roll out and follow them niggas" Yeah, "I hope that nigga enjoy that tit show" Andre said because it's his last one." "Oh shit! Look them niggas leaving early, and they got one of them stripper bitches with them." Andre said looking through the window.

# CHAPTER 57

"Let them niggas get in their whip and ride out." We going to follow them, and make it do what it do." said Andre. "You know we are going have to dead the bitch too" he said. "Hey if you get it, you get it" replied Rahim as they pulled out to follow Josh's car.

They followed Josh to the Upper West Side, over by Dyckman projects. They watched as Josh and his companions pulled over and parked on the street, and the three of them got out. Andre and Rahim pulled past them and parked a few cars ahead. They watched as the three got out the car laughing and talking loud. The two men had the stripper in the middle of them and Josh was palming her ass, as they walked towards the entrance of the project. "Let me go in there and see what apartment they go into" said Rahim, "dude don't know me" "I will send u a text alert to come inside the building and what floor to meet me on kid" Aight, that's good money replied Andre I'm going to crack this nigga, he been hiding up here in the projects all these time."

# CHAPTER 58

"Hit you in a sec" Rahim said as he opened the door to the car and walked quickly into the building. As he walked in Josh, the stripper and the second guy were standing waiting for the elevator. The three were laughing loudly. They turned around and looked at Rahim as he came up behind them. Josh looked at Rahim, trying to determine if he had seen him before, when the elevator dinged and the door slid open. Josh punched floor 6 as Rahim walked in after them. He said to Josh, pretending he hadn't seen which floor Josh pushed the button for and said could you push 6 please? "Yeah we got it money" Josh replied, his male companion said to the stripper, "so girl what kind of private show you going to put on for us, when we get to the crib", he slurred. She moved against him and rubbed his meat through his jeans. "Hey, that money was right, so ahh you can have whatever private show you want. Now that's what I'm talking about." said Josh "ass for rent, fuck em, and put them out" he sneered the elevator came to a stop and the doors opened. The three got off and Rahim got off behind them. They walked to apt 6b and Josh pulled out his keys, while the other two kept laughing and rubbing all over each other. Josh opened the door, Rahim had stopped in front of 6f and dropped down pretending that his shoe lace had become untied until they went inside the apt and shut the door.

# CHAPTER 59

Rahim walked to the elevator and got back on, as he went back to the first floor, he began to text Andre to tell him to meet him in the building lobby.

# CHAPTER 60

When Rahim came down to the first floor, he walked over to the entrance and waited until Andre came inside the hallway. "So what's up" Andre said as he came inside the building. They are upstairs on the 6th floor in apt 6b, they about to train the stripper chick, let's give them a minute to get more relaxed, so they will be totally unaware of what's about to go down" Rahim said. I got a key pick with me and you know up in here in the projects, the lock should be no problem to get open." Aight, give this nigga a min, let's wait in the car for a few, so we won't be to obvious standing in this hallway at 3:00 in the morning" Andre said. The two men walked outside and got in the car to wait. Taj, and Najah had finished their romantic dinner at their friend's restaurant, they had gone to a reggae club in Brooklyn and were on the way back to their hotel suite.

# CHAPTER 61

Najah had given one of the housekeeper instructions that right before midnight to go in their room and pull the bed covers back. The maid was also instructed to put rose petals from the bedroom door to the bed, where the petals were spread all over the bed. There were candles lit in candle stands around the bedroom. The housekeeper had also been instructed to fill the Jacuzzi up with bubbles, and turn the heating system on to keep the water warm. There was a bottle of "Dom" chilling in a bucket of ice. There were also candle stands in the bathroom that were lit as well. There was a collection of soft, and slow music for the couple when they got in the room. Taj, Najah and the security detail came into the hotel entrance, and as Najah had set up prior, the hotel manager came over and said there was a problem with the bill, and he needed Taj to clear it up. "Can't this wait man" Taj replied "me and my lady were about to take it in for the night." "Sir, it will only take a minute" the manager replied. Taj said alright man, come, Abdul you and Q take Najah up to the room I'll keep Fifo with me." Ok, she said as she smiled to herself to see that her plan was working out so well.

# CHAPTER 62

When she got up the suite, Abdul came in with her to make sure everything was cool. "Have a nice evening Ms Najah" he said as he turned to leave to go next door to the adjoining room. "Good night Abdul" she replied. Najah hurriedly took off her clothes making sure all of her instructions to the housekeeper were completed. There was a large bowl of strawberries and bananas and kiwi in it. There was also a large container of whipped cream on the night stand near the bed. She knew she only had a few minutes before Taj came up.

Najah walked into the bathroom and tested the water, she stood up and looked in the large mirror in the bathroom at her now naked body. Her firm 36C's stood at attention, her stomach was flat and concave, and her pussy was trimmed and neat. She took her long hair down out of the French knot she had in from earlier and let it hang down her back as Taj liked it.

# CHAPTER 63

The phone rang once letting her know Taj was on the way up. She went into the front room and put in a "Floetry" cd and poured two glasses "Dom" as she heard Taj's pass key at the door. As he opened it and saw the candle lit room, he said "oh shit" as he closed the door behind him, and Najah was standing there naked, with the two glasses in her hands. "Taj took in her body as she walked towards him and his dick got hard instantly. "Here you go baby" Najah said as she passed him a glass of champagne. "Happy anniversary again baby, I love you" she said as she kissed him. "Damn baby, when did you have time to do all this" Taj asked?

"I got my sources too" Najah replied and smiled at him. She put her glass down and began to unbutton his shirt. "I got a nice bath ready for us baby, so that we can do this correctly."

"I hear that ma" he replied as he drank his drink and watched Najah as she took off his clothes and led him into the bathroom.

# CHAPTER
# 64

"Floetry" cd was still playing softly in the bathroom that was lit up with thousands of candles. Najah walked over to the tub and felt the water. "Baby it's the right temperature, come over here and get this pussy" she said as she got into the bubbled water. "Damn" Taj said as he walked over to the Jacuzzi and stepped in behind Najah. Najah kneeled in the water as Taj got in, she refilled their glasses and handed him his glass. "To us baby, I love you so much papi" she said. "I love you too ma, more than anything" He said as he sipped from his glass and pulled Najah down onto his lap in the water. They began kissing slowly, then Taj said oh hold up baby, let me get us another drink. As he turned around in the tub after refilling the glasses, he said, let me put the cork back in. Taj gave the two glasses to Najah and turned back to the ice tub. "Damn! I think I dropped something in the ice bucket" Taj said. When he turned back around, he reached for his glass and while kneeling in front of Najah in the tub, he toasted to her saying. "Baby, for the moment I met you, I know you would be the mother of my children, I love you more than breath itself, will you marry me?" Taj asked Najah pulling the ring box from behind his back and giving the box to Najah, who began screaming with happiness. "Omg! Omg!" She exclaimed she dropped her glass in the tub of hot, bubbling water. "Yes, baby, I will marry you" Najah laughed, she opened up the ring box to reveal a 4.5 carat, platinum engagement ring. It was set in white and yellow gold. The diamond itself was flawless. Najah looked at the ring on her finger, before looking at Taj with tears in her eyes. 'I love you so much baby" and she kissed him on the mouth. Taj put his glass down on the side rim of the Jacuzzi where you could place items like soap, wine glass, etc. Taj picked up Najah's fallen glass out the water and put it next to his on the floor. He moved back closer to her and put his lips on hers. "I love you more baby" The flickering from the candles that were all over the bathroom, made a soft glow, music flowed into the bathroom softly. Taj started to suck at her breast, as he held her hips close.

# CHAPTER 65

Najah leaned her body back to allow him full access of her titties. "Ohh baby, that feels so good" she moaned as he continued to suck on her nipples. She put her hand under the water and began to massage his dick, which was already semi hard, she took her mouth from his and put it on his dick, she began to slowly lick and kiss the head of his huge dick. Taj moaned deep in his throat as he ran his fingers through her long hair, Taj reached behind her to palm her plump ass cheeks as she continued to make love to him with her mouth. After about ten minutes of this, she sat up on her knees again. She smiled at him and kissed him, before turning around to bare her ass cheeks to him. She turned and leaned over the edge of the Jacuzzi so that he could position himself behind her. "Damn you got a pretty ass ma" Taj said as he began to poke his swollen member around her opening, she moaned as Taj pushed inside her. He began to back stroke her slowly. Their moans filled the air, Taj slowly pulled out of her as he kissed the back of her neck while cupping her breast. "Baby lets switch up a bit, I want those titi's in my mouth." Taj said letting her go to let Najah climb up and sit on top of him. As she began to slowly ride him in the water, she passionately kissed him as she rode the dick. She sat up and Taj cupped both her breast and put them in his mouth. Taj began to suck her nipples like a baby would. Najah moaned out loud again. "Te amo bebé" Najah moaned (I love you baby)

# CHAPTER 66

Their bodies moved faster as the intensity increased, "Aww shit" Taj cried out "Damn baby this shit feel good as fuck, "I am about to come Naa, damn I want to come in this pussy." "So handle your business papi" Najah said as she continued to ride him, because I'm going to come with you" she moaned. Finally, they both cried out as they climaxed together. Najah collapsed on top of Taj's chest, his arms wrapped around her as they came down from exploding together.

# CHAPTER 67

Najah sat up, "baby let me wash you off a little something, and then we can take this into the bedroom." I got some desert in there, that I can feed to you, so you can give it to me again" she smiled. "Now that sounds like a plan to me mami" Taj replied . . ." that sounds like a plan to me.

Rahim and Andre had waited the 15 minutes and were walking back towards the building, they pulled ski mask over their faces, even though Dyckman projects was known for being a high crime area, where nobody talked and nobody ever saw anything. The two men clicked a chamber into their guns as they walked into the building putting them in the back of their jeans as they took the stairs this time, just to see who was hanging out in the stairwell at 3:30 in the morning. The stairway was deserted as they reached the 6$^{th}$ floor. "After I get the door open let's try to use our knives if we can to keep the shit quiet" Andre said, "if we gotta bust then, we bust."

"But we want to try and avoid that" he said. "I got you dog" Rahim replied, entering the 6$^{th}$ floor from the exit doorway.

# CHAPTER
# 68

Rahim and Andre looked up and down the hallway to make sure there was nobody out and then walked over to 6b. There was loud music playing from inside the apartment, "oh they partying up in this piece" Andre said, "this should make it a little easier because these niggas ain't going hear shit." Rahim took out the tool to insert in the key hole. He turned it clockwise until he heard the lock click they pulled their guns from their waist bands. "Let's do this" Rahim said. They slowly opened the apartment door, the living room area was dark, the music pumped from a stereo sound system on an entertainment center in the corner. There was no one in the, living room area. They walked down the hallway, where they could hear grunts and groans. "On a count of 3 Rahim" Andre whispered. Rahim nodded. They pushed open the door of the bedroom. Josh was lying on his back on the bed, and the stripper was riding his dick. The other dude was behind her fucking her in the ass. None of them saw Andre or Rahim enter as they continued their menage. Rahim threw his blade and buried it in the back of dude fucking the chick from the back. He fell over on the bed and his body hit the floor. Josh and the stripper and instantly set up in the bed. Andre rushed to the bed, and grabbed the chick by the throat. "Shut the fuck up bitch and you better not scream" he growled as he choked her. "You fucking hear me?" he said, she was shaking as she nodded yes. Andre threw her back on to the bed. Meanwhile, Josh tried to lunge up off the bed and run to the bedroom door. Rahim lifted up his arm and slammed it into Josh's throat slamming him to the floor. Andre looked at the stripper, "you better not fucking move off that bed he said to her "or you a dead bitch" Andre walked over to where Josh was laying on the floor, Josh eyes widened as he recognized Andre. "Yeah nigga" Andre said, "so your punk ass just thought you was going to do that shit to my little sister and walk away dog?" Andre asked as he bent down to be on the same level as Josh. "Look man" Josh started to say. "Shut the fuck up nigga, I don't want to hear nothing you have to say" Andre cut in, "you know what time it is", you played your cards wrong dog, you should have known eventually I was going to get your ass" he said as he pulled out some rubber gloves and then took out

a knife. "Come on man" Josh tried to talk "Shut the fuck up!! Andre said and he told Rahim to tie Josh up and lay him on his back on the floor and put some tape over his mouth. Once that was done Andre went over to Josh again and squatted next to the naked man, pulled up his now limp dick and cut it off. Josh began thrashing wildly around as blood squirted everywhere, Josh was screaming behind the tape that covered his mouth. In one hand Andre held what was left of Josh's dick and pulled out his gun and shot Josh in the chest. Andre then tore the tape off Josh's mouth and stuffed his dick in it. The stripper put her hands to her mouth, "bitch don't you do it" Rahim said to her. You just happened to be at the wrong place at the wrong time and shot her point blank in the face. "Let's go nigga somebody probably heard those shots." Rahim said.

The stripper fell down onto the bed naked and spread eagle. The two men looked around the room and then making sure all three of the targets were dead and they silently left the apartment. The two men walked back out the building and towards Andre's car, "Yo! I am hungry dog", Andre said lets go up to Jimbo's on 135th and get some of them thick ass burgers and some fries." "Yeah I'm wit dat" Rahim replied, "let's bounce" They got in the car and drove uptown.

# CHAPTER
# 69

Meanwhile, Sin was up at The Org's spot up on White Plains road, he was doing a count of the weekly money that came in from the lieutenants that ran River Park. The dollar amount on the money counting machine read $85,000 it should have read $90, 000. So somebody is trying to be slick. The amount of work that they had coming through this spot was crazy so Sin and Taj tried to make sure everybody was sharing in the wealth, and "nigga's still gotta steal, Sin thought to himself. He got up from the desk and checked the inventory sheet to see which cash drops had been done for the night. Everybody had logged in except for the crew on 205$^{th}$ street. He looked at the log from last week, they came in last week also and they were short 4g's. What the fuck! He said he pulled out his cell phone and called the lieutenant that should have been on top of this, especially it being the second week in a row that these niggas been coming up short. The phone rang till it went a voice message. Yo! "Kid this Sin, I need you to return this call asap because shit ain't looking too good over here, I got a two weeks of shortage and aint nobody telling me or Taj shit."

"Hit me back like yesterday nigga." He banged the phone close he opened the door to the office and called downstairs to where two of the night lieutenants were playing cards. "Rock, come up here for a second dog." As Rock came into the room, Sin sat back behind the desk, "close the door" he told Rock. "Can you explain to me, you being the nigga here in charge at night why these niggas from 205$^{th}$ come up $4,000 short last week and this week no drop at all and nobody thought to inform me or Taj" he asked. Yo Rock started to say, "Nah nigga just give me the short version" Sin said to him "cause that's all I want to hear", Just then Sin's phone vibrated, "yo hold up nigga", he said to Rock as he picked up the phone and looked at the "caller id". "What's up ma? Oh word, that's what's up. Listen I am right in the middle of some real, real important shit, I am going to hit you back soon as" Sin said. "Thank you baby" he clicked the cell phone shut and looked at Rock. "Now you was saying" "That nigga Big been sending other niggas to drop off the money from 205th the last two times, they dropped off their paper for the weekly count." The first time he aint show, he sent C-Note and that kid Razor." When I asked where Bigg was, they were like he had an emergency out of town with his moms, and that he would call me that night.

## CHAPTER 70

"The nigga never called, nor did he answer his cell the next day." Rock said, then this week, the same thing happens, the same two niggas." "Wait! hold up nigga, so why is it the Friday night, the second week of this shit and aint nobody called me or Taj and told us shit!" Sin interrupted. "This shit is unacceptable for a nigga in your position with The Organization so now that makes me question you too." Sin said, "Sin, hold up Sin, I was going to tell you but you asked me to handle that shit on the two new dudes" I aint get shit back on that nigga Rahim, something not right with that, there is no word on dude on the street, nowhere, he said he did some work with Ock and them niggas in Bklyn., but I aint hear nothing back on that." And you came through before I could tell about this shortage shit with Bigg." The other kid, Andre checked out though he little wild, that nigga definitely put in work in the street." Hold up" Sin said as he took out his cell phone and dialed a number, "Yo Bigg, what up nigga, yeah, I am at the spot, there seems to be a little misunderstanding over here to the tune of 9 grand." Your crew was short 4gs last week and this week and you send some other niggas here without notice?" What's up with that? You know the rules nigger, and if you had an emergency, why you aint call and check in with me or Taj?" And most importantly where the fuck is the money you short?" Sin listened then he said into the phone "make it an hour Bigg not one minute later, tonight, not tomorrow, one hour with the money." He hung up and said to Rock, that nigga Bigg is supposed to be here in an hour, I want you to wait and get that paper from him." If he does not show, fuck calling in an hour, you call me immediately." Sin said I got some shit to handle up town and I am going to see some people about that nigga Rahim." Sin turned to walk out the door with his two security detail stopped and looked at Rock, don't ever make the decision to not tell me about when my money is funny . . . never or it will come off your cut" he said and walked out the door. "Stupid ass motherfuckers" Sin said to his bodyguards as they walked out to the car.

# CHAPTER 71

The two detail guys look both ways before the three men walked towards the parked Explorer Sin clicked his phone open, as the detail guys reached to open the truck door, a black SUV sedan came speeding towards them, "get down! one of the security detail yelled as he pushed Sin over towards the passenger side of the Explorer and down to the ground, pulling out his gun in the other hand. The second body guard ducked down and ran over to the passenger side of the SUV as well. His gun was already pointed toward the SUV that was heading right for them. The windows slid open and two niggers one, in the back window and one in the front passenger side, stuck their heads out that wearing black hoods and their faces covered with mask. The men in the fast approaching sub cocked back on the semi automatic weapons they both held, and started spraying gunfire. Bullets sprayed the windows of Sin's car, but the bullets bounced off the bullet protected windows. Sin rolled under the Explorer pulling his gun from out the small of his back, he could hear the screech of the SUV as it roared past them spraying gunfire. One of the bodyguards dropped down to eye level with Sin, "you alright chief?" he asked "come up from under there, we gotta move quick cause we don't know if these punk ass niggas going try and roll back around." he said as he helped Sin from under the vehicle. The other guard had the door opened and looking up the street and back he got into the driver's side and they sped off. "What the fuck! Sin as they sped down the street, "can somebody tell me what the fuck was that shit?" "I don't know dog, said the driver as he looked in the review mirror at Sin and then checked for cars behind to make sure they were not being followed. "But I know I have never seen them around before, but dude in the back window, had a large tattoo of a panther on his hand." I seen that shit clear as day" "A panther? Sin said, he looked at the guard in the passenger seat, "Abu get on your horn and put your little street on that shit." I want to know who this niggas is by tonight." Tell the nigga that get these dudes got at me and whoever brings them to me gets $10,000." Get on that shit right now." Sin said to Abu, as he clicked open his phone, and set up an emergency meeting at the "roundtable" which was an unknown location except for those high up in The Organization.

# CHAPTER
# 72

"I'm on it" Malcolm, the second security detail answered. Sin spoke into his phone, My nigga, yeah I think we got a little situation, some niggers just tried to roll on us, yeah Yo! leaving the spot. After I got finished getting in that nigga Rock's ass, cause the weekly count was short a couple of thousand, that little fat fuck Biggs." Yo Taj, this nigga been short a couple grand for the last two weeks and today was the first day I'm hearing about this shit." Nah, I gave the nigga an hour to bring it to the spot, and told that nigga Rock, to call me either way it goes." This is crazy with all this shit going on lately first you and your girl, now this shit." I think we should get the girls out the city and beef up security a little til we get this shit handled." Which reminds me, I gotta call my girl back before she hear about the shit on the street and start tripping you know how that street shit goes. Her peeps got ears to the street out here like that, you know how that street shit go.

# CHAPTER 73

"Meet you at the spot, in a half, keep your eyes and ears open Taj, this is two incidents in the past 24, first at your crib, and now this shit." I don't want to have to kill a whole borough if something happens to you my dude, I'm out" Sin, punched in a number to call his girl, to tell her to get some things together.

Across town four masked men were speeding down a darkened street, reached an abandoned warehouse and pulled up in front. "Yo kill the fucking headlights" one of the guys said as they got out the truck, and began pulling off their masks, and taking off their black jumpsuits and throwing them in the truck. 'This shit if is fucked up, we didn't even get the job done, that nigger Sin still breathing, and that shit don't look good B." I don't like when my money gets fucked." "Get all that shit inside the truck and light that shit up, leave no traces of nothing behind." The sub was set on fire and the four men ran towards a parked sedan and got in and sped off.

Taj, and Najah had just finished looking at a mini mansion in the Paramus, NJ, the property was surrounded by a high fenced in gates. It had 5 large bedrooms, with a large spacious living room area there was a large Olympic sized pool, with a guest house in the back. "I love the house baby" Najah said "there is so much I can do with the decorations, when we come back from visiting my family." Taj broke in," ahh Najah baby, there has been a little change of plans, something really important has come up, and I need to stay here and handle it, you and Monet will go out there first and me and Sin will follow behind in a couple of days." "Baby, what's going on?" Najah asked is something to do with what happened at the house." "Baby stop asking so many questions alright mamie, I got this, I will have some our stuff moved to the new place, the furniture and shit we will buy everything new and I just want you to get ready to leave, tomorrow, call your grandparents and tell them, you will be there two days early." Najah, walked over to Taj and put her finger to his lips to silence him. 'Baby, just remember to please guard your back and stay focused on us and our plans baby, Just live off the companies, and the other business's we have, get married, have babies, and growing old together, you know all that good shit." she removed her finger from his lips and kissed and then hugged him. "Please be careful baby, I got a bad feeling, and something is not right" she said to him. "Don't worry baby, everything is going to be fine I love you and we going to have that family baby now, just get packed, don't pack a lot of shit, I will give you some extra money to shop while you out there." Taj said. "Sin and I are going to take you ladies to the airport, in the morning. So let's get moving baby. Y'all plane leave at 7:45am tomorrow to San Jose, it will arrive there at 6:45pm. So call your grandparents and let them know the times baby and I'll be back. I just got to go and check some things out and then I am going to take you out for dinner. I gotta meet with Sin real quick and then I'll be back ok?" Taj hugged and kissed her again and left the room. As soon as Taj left the room, Najah, picked up her cell phone and punched a button, "hola, abeula" "I am going to speak English" Najah said to her grandmother, Just me and Sin's girl, Monet is coming out tomorrow instead of Friday. Taj, and his guest will not be coming until the weekend. Can you send someone pick us up from the airport, we should arrive at 6:45 pm in Costa Rica. I will send you the flight number info later on. I will explain when I get there Abuela, I love you bye." Najah, put the phone down, she sat down on the bed, she was still thinking about the break in at the house, and the men that tried to kill her. She didn't want to upset her grandmother by telling her on the phone, she would wait until she saw her and her grandfather when she reached the island. She clicked the phone again, "what's up little mama" she said into the phone, did you tell Sin about the baby yet?" "I'm going to be an auntie" Najah squealed into the phone. "I hope you have a little girl too that will be the shit." although knowing Sin ass, he want a little man. "Listen Monet, something is going on but Taj is all hush, hush and shit and all of sudden you and me leaving tomorrow without them.' I am just going to put a few things in a little carryall set I got, Taj gave me money to go shopping when we get down there, but I got a bad feeling about shit." Well go ahead finish your packing and get ready for your little surprise night to your hubby, I will talk to you in the morning. One"

Najah got up and put a couple of things into her baby phat, carryall, she threw some undies in there. Eveything else she would get once she arrived at the capital city. She turned on the shower, but then remembered she had to do a few small errands before relaxing for the night. Once again, her mind went back to the night before events. She remembered the last time she and her grandfather talked he had told her that there was a family meeting that he wanted her to be at. Something to do with the holdings and different accounts he had set up in her and her sister's name when they become the age of 24. Najah, would be 24 in a month, Maria still had eight years to go. She sighed again as she picked up her long hair in the back and pinned it up with a clip as she adjusted the water. At least, she could spend some time with her sister and find out what's going on with her. The last couple of times they talked, Maria had rushed her off the phone, always promising to call back and never did. Najah finished her shower, and dried off. She put a night slip on, and clicked on the tv. She yawned and picked up her cell phone again. "Baby, why don't we order and you bring it with you when you come." We can eat in bed, I love you too baby." She hung up the phone. This would be the first time, that Najah's grandparents had met Taj, and Najah wanted everything to go well with this visit.

# CHAPTER
# 74

In Brooklyn Sin, Taj, Rock and some of the other lieutenants were playing pool in the basement. They had met at one of their neutral spots, where they came to meet, and chill for a second. It was a large brownstone, they had bought the whole building and had it renovated, by one of those urban city project programs, in their mother's names, who both owned their own small businesses. Sin, lit a blunt, and then bent over the pool table to shoot his shot. Taj, was sitting on a stool watching Sin play, Jadakiss, "U Make Me Wanna" was playing. "So what's the deal with this kid Biggs man", Taj asked Rock. "Dude never called in the hour that he was supposed to" Rock replied. I called his phone, and got the voice mail. I called his sister crib to see if she could get me some info on the nigga, and the bitch claimed she aint seen him." But the funny thing is that right after that shit happened today with Sin, somebody called the office phone and asked was everything ok, I asked who the fuck it was, but they didn't answer, so I hung up." Rock said, but now that I'm thinking about it, why would somebody call and say that, and then that shit go down like that. Now only a few of us know the office number to that particular spot." Me, the 5 of us here and Biggs." Sin stood up with the pool stick in his hands. "And this nigger been short the last couple of weeks" he said. Get some of the men together, I want two teams, one go to dude mother crib and sniff around and shit, send the other team, up to that chick that nigga was fucking up in Harlem. That stripper bitch, get her to talk, this nigga got too much mouth to stay out of sight for long." And if this nigger is behind this shit, like my gut is saying he's fucking dirt bag." Taj cut in. before anybody does anything call me or Sin first I want something, better yet someone bought back here tonight. Sin and me gotta go and get do some shit, but I want a full report, or the niggas responsible bought to us at the spot." And Rock, bring in Turtle and his crew, I want this shit done correctly." Taj said "Nobody disrespects The Organization Turtle unlike his name was a vicious killer that The Organization used from time to time for special jobs, and this shit tonight with Sin, and the shit at my house the other day . . . gotta be handled with no questions asked." So fellas, any questions before we break up outta here." Sin asked. "Nah we good dog" Rock answered "I'll give you the call in a couple of hours, whichever way the wind blows." The men slapped hands, and Sin, Taj and the bodyguards left the building. Taj an Sin Stood talking outside for a minute, their bodyguards were standing spaced out in front, watching the street for any suspicious movement. "Listen my dude, we going just lay low a couple of days, the woman will be out of town til we handle this shit", Taj said, we should be able to wrap this shit up and meet them down there later this weekend." The two men shook hands and did the man hug thing, and got into their cars, with security in the cars with them and each had a security car trailing each of them.

# CHAPTER 75

Over in Bed Sty section of Brooklyn Najah, had just come out of a warehouse storage unit that she had rented when she and Taj had decided to move in together. As far as he knew it was some old furniture that she told him was heirlooms, but what he didn't know was that she also had a change of clothes, several thousands of dollars in cash, and several semi automatic weapons, with ammo. There was even some fake id's for her and Taj, thanks to her grandfather's connects. She had placed these items just in case they ever had to flee the country. Taj didn't know how powerful a man grandfather was, nor her background, or the fact that she was trained to kill at will. That was another side of her life that she kept totally hidden. One day she would tell him, and the things that she had done in the name of her family, but she would do so in her time. She quickly put two 9 mm in the small carry bag, that she had bought with her, and some clips, she also threw in a couple of stacks of cash, it never hurt to have extra for emergencies. She had over a million dollars stashed here, not counting money she had put away over the years in offshore accounts. She also pulled out small holster with a knife attached to it, and strapper it around her leg. Since they were flying in one of her grandfather's jet, she didn't have to worry about security checking her for weapons or illegal substances. She closed the gate down and locked it. She walked quickly over to her Mercedes Benz SL, it was starting to get dark, and she wanted to get to jersey before Taj came home. The security detail was waiting parked behind her car. They got out the car as she came out of the storage room, and walked over to escort her to her car. They opened the door for her, and as she got behind the wheel, her cell went off, she looked at the caller id, it was Taj. "Hey baby, what's up, everything ok?" she asked him.: Yeah shit copasetic, me and Sin finishing up here and I are about to come to the room and chill with my baby for the rest of the night." Taj replied what you want to eat?"

"Baby could you please stop by our favorite restaurant and bring me a platter, you know what I like from Sylvia's." Najah said. I just had to run out and get some last minute toiletries and items I will need for my trip. Now I am on the way back to the suite, and yes baby before you ask me, security is right behind me." "Alright, I love you, be careful." Taj said and they hung up the line. She clicked the phone shut and put it on her clip. Traffic wasn't so bad, so she would be in Teaneck in no time. She wanted to shower and get the things she had gotten from the storage unit packed up with the rest of her things that she was taking to Costa Rica. As she pulled up to the lavish hotel, the bellman came over to her and opened the door. "May I help you with your bags Ms. Najah?" The bellman asked as he signaled to another bellman to come help with Najah's things. The four security detail and Najah walked over to the elevators, and they went inside as the doors were about to close, two men tried to get on the elevator, the two security in the front stepped up, and said to them," take the next one, this one is full." The two men looked at the security detail that had their hands in their coats ready to fire at will and stepped back. "No problem my man" As they got off on the penthouse floor, Najah told the security she was going to take a shower and then should be on the way shortly. Two of the detail walked with her to her door and posted out front. The other two went into the suite directly next door. Najah went inside and she finished packing the small items she was taking, she threw in the weapons and clips and the two stacks of money. She took off her clothes and went turned the shower on, while pulling her hair up in a ponytail. Najah stepped into the hot water that cascaded down her body, she soaped herself up good rinsed off and got out the shower. Najah oiled her body down with some lightly scented bath and body works oil, and put on Victoria Secret lingerie set, that she never worn for Taj. She turned on the TV and got onto to the large king size bed. She flicked on the news, there was talk about a drive by shooting that took place in the Flatbush section of Brooklyn earlier that evening, as she sat and watched the news reporter she noticed the news showed the vehicles that were involved in the shootout earlier. Although they were being tagged and fingerprinted by police Najah recognized Sin's Explorer. "Oh shit, that looks just like Sin's car" she said to herself, she listened intently to the news. The police had yet to find clues to who did it or motives. "So this is the shit, Taj was trying to hide from me earlier' Najah thought to herself. "No wonder he wanted me and Monet to leave town early" she mused. Najah clicked off the news and turned on some soft music. She finished getting undressed for bed and put her overnight bag in the front foyer of the large suite she and Taj were staying at until the paperwork for their new house was finalized. This was two incidents in the space of 24 hours, Najah couldn't stop her mind from wondering to what the fuck was going on, she knew her grandfather had ears everywhere, if anybody could information, he could. She went and turned down the lights outer room so Taj could see coming into the suite. Najah went and lay down on the bed, she loved listening to Floetry but tonight she opted to go with some Maxwell. As she lie across the bed, and let the music sooth her racing thoughts, she fell asleep.

# CHAPTER 76

Meanwhile on the other side of the city, Sin was walking into his crib, he could hear the sounds of music playing as he walked into the large marble covered foyer, and threw his keys on the table. He looked the mail that was laying there and threw it back down, aint nothing there but fucking bills no way he thought to himself. He punched the alarm code and walked into the dining room area "Monet, baby where you?" Sin called out "I am in the dining room baby" Monet responded back. Sin walked into the dining room area. The large highly polished wood table was set for two, there were candles on the table, and a large bottle of champagne was chilling on ice. Monet was undressed in a two piece black see through teddy. Her perfect size 38C's peeked through the lace of the black teddy. She had on black lace thong panties, her ass was round and plump. Her back was to him as she taking the steamed plates from the tray that was next to the dining room table. She smiled at him, 'hey baby" she said as she put the hot plants on the table. "Damn! I love her body Sin thought to himself looking at her as she walked over to him and gave him a kiss. "I missed you daddy" she said as she rubbed her body against his. His arms encircled hers, and he hugged her close and inhaled her smell. She smelled sweet, like lavender. He winced a little bit as he hugged Monet tight, his shoulder was still sore from earlier when he had to roll under the truck earlier, but he didn't want to say anything about what happened to Monet just yet. Taj and Sin had decided to keep the shit on lock what had happened earlier, otherwise there was no way the girls would leave tomorrow. "So what's the occasion?" he said nodding to the champagne chilling. "Stop being so fast" she said. Let's sit down and eat something first, and enjoy this night, since me and Najah leaving in the morning." She led him over to the table where she had placed the plate. She uncovered the top and there was steamed lobster tails, broiled scallops, fresh broccoli and NY strip steak well done, just the way he liked it. She walked back over to the tray, and bought the bowl of cesear salad, and placed it on the table. She got the other hot steaming plate and put it down, the room was lit dimly, the room smelled of the large area of fresh flowers that sat in the middle of the table. "This looks good baby, you definetly know how to make a nigga a home, he said, so where did you order from cause I know you ain't had time to make all these shit, by the time your ass finished all your last minute shopping" Sin laughed. Monet, threw her napkin at him, ohh hush and just eat" she laughed. It's all good baby Sin said, I know you can burn, you got all the qualities I want in my wife besides being able to fuck the shit out of me all night." Sin laughed, I want you to be my wife for real ma, he looked at her, I want you to be the mother of my seeds, I love you baby." Sin said. "Aww I love you too daddy, forever Monet cried. "Sin took the bottle of champagne from the bucket and popped the cork, he poured a glass for the both of them. "Here's to us baby" with a little minor details, were finally about to have everything we ever wanted." Sin said. He leaned over the table and kissed Monet on the lips. Monet smiled at the man, who she loved to death and she said, "While we toasting, I want to make another toast" she said, she reached under the table and bought out a small gift bag and put it on the table. Sin looked at the bag, "aww shit, what's that baby? He asked. "Just open it" Monet said. Sin reached inside the bag and pulled out a large envelope, and opened it, inside was a sonogram which at the top read the name 'Donate twins". He looked at the picture and looked at Monet again. "Baby is this what I think it is he said as he stood up smiling. "Yep you are going to be a daddy . . . . daddy" Monet said, we are having a set of twins, the doctors said it's too early to tell the sex of the babies, but its definitely two them in there" she said. Sin came around the table to where Monet sat and hugged her, "damn girl, I am about to be a father yeah!! Sin shouted and laughed. He rubbed her still flat stomach, damn ma, we getting ready to have two babies, maybe boys, maybe girls, but we going be parents now, damn no more fucking around, this some real shit" he said. He picked her up from the seat gently and carried her to their bedroom, Monet had the room totally lit with candles, there were fresh rose petals scattered across the large king size bed, canopied bed. He laid her gently down on the bed and lay down next to her. He looked in her eyes, "Monet, baby will you be my wife?" I wasn't planning on proposing tonight, but in light of becoming an impending father, this shit gotta be official. You can pick out whatever diamond you want ma" he said. When me and Taj meet yall down there this weekend, I will place it on your finger the proper way." Tears started streaming down Monet's face as she smiled. "Yes baby, I love you so much." Sin kissed her softly and slid his fingers into her thong strap, he began to and slowly pulls them down, he stuck his fingers inside her wetness. He took of her top and began to slowly lick her large nipples. She moaned out loud. Monet had a bowl of fresh strawberries and whipped cream in a bowl on the side of the bed. Sin got up and bought the bowl of strawberries and cream in the bed with them. He took out one large strawberry and pulled the stem off of it, he then parted Monet's legs slowly and put the strawberry inside her dripping pussy. She moaned again, "I'm about to make my own split" he said as he took the spoon and began to put the whipped cream around Monet's pussy lips. Damn baby" she moaned, Sin bent down and began to eat Monet's pussy like it was a meal, he ate the strawberry and began to lick the cream in large slurping noises. Monet began to moan louder, "daddy, I wanna feel that dick" she moaned, "give it to me now" Sin came up from her pussy, his face was wet with her juices and traces of the whip cream, he stood up off the bed, and began to strip off his clothes slowly, he knew Monet loved his ripped body. He smiled as he gyrated his hips a little as "R Kelly's "Whine for me" played in the background As he took off his pants and his boxers, his large, thick dick was rock hard, and stood at attention. Monet began to rub her titties as she watched Sin come back towards the bed, only he could make her feel so freaky, horny and wet all at the same time. He slid up over her body and she raised her hips to receive him inside her. Sin moaned as he slid into her tight pussy. "Damn baby, my pussy tight, this shit feel so fucking good." He groaned. Monet's legs wrapped around his hips and he began to move slowly inside her. "Ahhhh, ahhh" she panted as he moved inside her pussy, she gripped his shoulders as they both lost themselves in the feeling that was overtaking them both. They were both moaning and breathing hard, "I want to ride this dick daddy" Monet said breathlessly as they changed positions. She straddled his large dick and began to rock on it slowly. She moved back and forth slowly as Sin sat halfway up on the pillows and began to suck he breast. He cupped her ass as he moaned and they both began to move faster and faster together. They both exploded at the same time, and Monet collapsed on top of Sin's chest. His arms enclosed around her body, neither of them saying anything, just enjoying the aftermath of the sex they just had. "Baby, we going to have a baby" Sin said in wonder, damn I got that super sperm" he laughed. "Shut up boy" she laughed as she playfully hit his chest. "We better plan this wedding quick before I start getting to big." Monet said.

"Yeah, we will talk about it when I see you this weekend, something with just our family and closet friends, we can even do something here at the house" Sin said. "This shit is big enough" he laughed. "Well will see baby she said. "I will be right back baby" she said "Where you going" he asked? "Right to the bathroom, she got up and came back a few minutes later, she had a small sponge bowl, in it was warm water and a small bar of soap and a small sponge, she bent down over her man, and began to slowly sponge him down, with the warm soapy water. "Mmm he moaned, "that feel good ma" he said. "You know I got you daddy" she said, as she cleaned him up. She put the sponge bowl down next to the bed, and she leaned over and took his still semi hard dick in her mouth. She knew her head game was crazy, and she loved sucking Sin's dick, she loved everything about his body she thought as she took him deep in her mouth. "Shit he moaned and she began to slurp his dick up and down, while lightly fingering his balls. His dick became rock hard in her mouth and she slurped that shit like it was an ice pop. She came up began circling the head with just her tongue, then engulfing him again completely in her mouth. "Daaamn" he said again, as he felt his toes began to curl from the shit. "Come ma, before your ass gonna make me cum" he said? He pulled her up and rolled her over on her stomach, he put a pillow under her lower stomach and spread her legs, he licked her ass and stuck his tongue inside her pussy. It smelt good, Monet had some good smelling ass pussy, he though and he slid up and slid inside her. She moaned as his dick slid in and out of her wet pussy. 'Ahhhh, ahhh" she moaned "Daddy, I love this dick" she panted. Sin was stroking the pussy harder and harder he knew he was about to nut and his shoulder was starting to throb a little. "Baby, I am about to come in this pussy" he moaned, "come on ma get that second nut" he panted. He put his hands under to grab and titties and began to squeeze her nipples. Monet began to thrust back against his dick feeling that buildup before she came. "Mmmm mmm mmm' Sin moaned as he felt his nut coming, he squeezed her nipples harder and began stroking her pussy harder. "Shit! Shit!" he shouted "I'm about to cum baby" Sin said. Monet ground her pussy on his dick harder so she could come with him. When the explosion came, this time Sin collapsed on her back before remembering about the babies in her stomach, he didn't want to lay on his heavy body and risk doing something to his seed. He slid off her and on to the bed, and rolled over and pulled her into his arms. She snuggled in them, "I love you husband" she smiled. "Mmmm Monet Donate" I liked that name" she said. "Yeah, I like that name too baby" Sin replied holding her close. His cell phone that was laying on the night stand began to vibrate. "Aww baby" Monet began "Shh give me second baby, this might be Taj, there is a little something that I got to handle, but it should only take an hr at the most, and its important baby, real important." "Then I'll be back to spend the rest of the night with you baby, I promise." Sin picked up his cell phone and clicked it open, "Yo, whats good with you my nigga, so what' s up with fat boy?" he asked into the phone, yeah alright, nah just chilling with my wifey, yeah I proposed to her my nigga, and check this fly shit, I am about to be a dad, of motherfucking twins.' Sin said into the phone, yeah alright I'll tell her, I'll see you there." He clicked the phone shut, baby, that was Taj, he said he love you and congratulations, like I said ma, I will be back, soon, he kissed her . . . "mmm that was some good loving" he said, 'I will see you and continue where we left off when I get back." He said.

Sin replied as he went and jumped in the shower real quick to go and meet Taj. After Andre and Rahim finished their business for the night, they said they would meet the next day at the spot. Andre dropped Rahim off at his crib, and jumped on the BQE. He clicked on his cell phone and dialed a number, yeah, this is Riggs, I am turning in for the night, nah I just dropped him off, he is a little on the wild side but dude a straight up thug, I did get to meet the famous Sin and Taj today, yeah it will all be in my report in the morning. Yes sir goodnight" he clicked the phone shut.

# CHAPTER
# 77

Meanwhile over at Andre's crib, he had walked inside and started taking off his clothes, he sat on the large sofa sectional and began to roll a blunt. "Babe you here, he called out, I'm in the bedroom, be there in a minute a voice called from the bedroom. Aight, hurry up and get your fine ass out here, he growled in his deep voice. He thought about the nights work, that shit at the warehouse with The Organization was just the beginning of what Andre aspired to be, paid for Andre had no soul, he was a stone cold killer. He had sliced one of his mother's sexual customers across the face, when he was just 10 years old when the john tried to beat his mother out of her money. Andre never knew his father it could have been any of the countless tricks his mother slept with. He grew up in the mean streets of Harlem, where you took or got taken. He went in the kitchen, his wife was at the stove cooking he picked her up and kissed her and told her he would be right back. Andre was a big dude, about 240lbs of solid muscle you wouldn't think he had a secret fetish for boys. He knocked on the door and Tyrique his secret boy toy of about one year, opened the door. Andre looked behind him to make sure no one saw him going inside, because of his life style, and especially being a lieutenant in the Organization, Andre knew he would be killed if anyone ever found out about him. After the sex was over, Andre got up and went into the bathroom to wash off. He came out zipping his pants and said to Tyrique. "Yo! I gotta bounce but here is some paper before I roll" Andre said. I'm about to run to the store and get a blunt, I'll see later. "Aight boo" Tarique replied. As Andre walked to the store to get some Dutches and as he got closer, he noticed a group of four men coming out the store, the men were talking loud amongst each other and didn't notice Andre as they walked towards a black Durango with tinted windows.

Andre looked real hard at one of the men, it was dark but thought he recognized one of them, but couldn't place him so he continued into the store. As he was paying for his Dutches, the store doorbell rang and Andre looked up to see Biggs walking into the store. Biggs didn't see Andre at first until it was too late, but Andre saw him "I knew I knew this nigga" Andre said as he pulled out his gun and told the clerk to shhhh. He crept up behind Biggs and hit him in the head with the gun. Shouting "Don't' you owe some money nigga?!!" Biggs was dazed from the hit to the head, Andre hit him again, and said "Oh we in the right aisle, duct tape is just what I need right now as he snatched a roll off the shelf." He kicked Biggs and quickly taped his arms and mouth up. Andre kicked him again and said "Get off the floor and walk your punk ass out the door. Andre's car was parked right in front of the store, and he pushed Biggs towards the passenger side and threw him in the car. He quickly ran over to the driver's side, jumped in and tore away from the curb. Andre commenced to beating Biggs with one hand, while driving with the other. As Andre got to a red light, he looked in the rear view mirror and saw the black Durango that had been parked in front of the store a bit ago and it was coming behind him fast. Andre picked up his cell and called Taj and said "Yo! Taj, I got that nigga Biggs in my car right now taped, but I'm being followed. I believe it's his crew I'm on the way to the warehouse now dog, I need some back up, get ready. Taj responded back on the other line. "We got you dog, bring him to me." Taj immediately called Sin, "Baby boy, we about to go to war, Andre found Biggs and is on the way here and he's being followed. I got some niggas here, but we need you." Sin responded "Aight, one!!

# CHAPTER 78

"Meanwhile at The Org" Taj went downstairs where a few of the men were in the sound proof basement. The basement was hooked with a large pool table, there was a 52inch Sony TV. A large sectional leather couch sat against one wall, there was a fully stocked bar on the other side. Some of the men were shooting pool some was playing the Play station 2 system that was hooked up to the large screen television. The men were standing by waiting for the word of when it was time to go to war. It came down the wire that someone had tried to kill the bosses wife, somebody was about to die. As Taj came running down the stairs he sounded the alarm. "It's time for war, strap up my niggas."

All you could see was niggas moving fast towards the stairs, strapping on vest, guns and grenades. Everybody got into position as the security alarm sounded throughout the building. Taj saw Andre on the monitor driving full speed towards the warehouse. He told the men to hold their position. Taj saw the black Durango as well, following closely behind Taj went into a busy open shopping area I Brooklyn, parked the car, and got out. He wore gloves, this was no chance coming at him with that finger print/DNA bull shit. He looked and saw the Durango was about 20 feet away from him. They screeched to a halt and four men jumped out the truck and starting bussing. Andre got hit in the stomach and once to the chest. He falls to the ground as the warehouse doors and windows open up and gun shots started ringing out at the four men. One of the men from the Durango yells out. "Ambush! He yelled as he gets popped in the head and falls to the ground. The other three men had been hit by the barrage of bullets and didn't even stand a chance. It was over just as Sin pulls up Taj comes out the front door and runs over to Andre. "Yo! Dog! Dog! You alright?" Andre was still alive but bleeding heavily. Taj told some of the men to get him to the hospital. Sin runs to the passenger side where Biggs was slumped over, dead. "Shit!! Sin said while going through Biggs pockets, these nigga got 20 g's.

Sin, Taj and some of the men walked over to inspect the dead bodies that were lying on the ground. Sin said "Yo! That's one of the niggas that tried to murk me earlier, with that tattoo on his hand. So Biggs was behind that shit?" Sin asked. "That's fucked up." Taj responded, yeah but we gotta clean this shit up, and get these bodies out of here." We can send the detail over and pay the cops off for not responding to the gun shots. Have the rest of these niggas clean this shit up." I'm about to bounce, and yo ass should too." "I'm out" Sin responded. "One" About two hours after the shootout, Taj finally got to Jersey. Traffic had been heavy. He told the security detail to stay posted outside the door, and Taj, went in. He had already spoken with the security detail to make sure they were ready to go by 5:00 am, to take the girls to the landing strip in the morning. In his hands he had and Najah"s food, collard greens, candied yams, baked Mac and cheese and baked chicken for her, short ribs for Taj. He went in and put the plates down on the dining room table, took off his gun holster and walked into the bedroom. He put his holster, gun and his keys down on the table and looked towards the bed. Najah was laying on her stomach fast asleep, she had on a red thongs, that showed off her rounded ass to perfection, and a red sheer, Victoria Secret nightie. He loved this woman, although he knew there were still some things in her past that she had yet to share with him. He knew in time she would. He knew everything else about her. And at some point soon he would marry her and have babies. He walked over to the bed, in the dimly light room, Najah's beautiful face shone in the candlelit. Her long hair framed the side of her face. He bent down and kissed her softly on the cheek, he couldn't stop his hand from cupping her soft ass. She murmured in her sleep and tuned over. 'Hey baby" she said sleepily and held her arms up for Taj to lay down with her. She closed him in her arms. "Le eché de menos papi" she whispered in his ear (I missed you papi). "I missed you too ma" Taj replied, I got your food that you wanted, and then I want you for desert" he smirked.

She sat up and smiled sexily at him as she kissed his lips again and got up and sat on his lap. They kissed deeply for a minute, before she got up and turned towards the dining area and gave him a beautiful view of her big brown ass. "She turned around and winked at him, "the faster we go eat, the faster I can eat you" she said to him as she turned and walked into the dining room laughing. "Oh I am with that ma, for sure" Taj replied as he got up and followed her out of the bedroom. They sat down at the table and began taking the food out the bags. "So you and Sin going be right behind us, right baby?" Najah asked. "Your business shouldn't keep you here to long right" she asked. She was thinking about what she had seen on the news earlier involving Sin's car. But she kept it to herself. She wanted to see if Taj would say anything in reference to what happened earlier. "Yeah baby, we will be right behind you ladies, its just some things that need to be handled right away." Taj replied. Najah didn't say anything she knew how close mouthed Taj could be at times about business. It irritated the fuck out of her at times, because she loved him. Najah still had not told him of her true family background and what a powerful man her grandfather was all over. She knew the time to tell him was soon at hand. All that he knew is that her grandfather was a business man in imports and had done very well for himself. "Najah" Taj called, "damn baby where you go, you just kind of drifted off for a minute." he laughed. She smiled at him as she ate her greens. "Shut up" she said so did you hear the news about Sin and Monet having twins?" "Yeah that nigga told me." He on cloud nine and shit" Taj laughed. "We going be an auntie and uncle until we make our own bambinos" Najah said "Yeah it's gonna happen ma, once I met your family and make it official, and didn't that 4 carat diamond ring seal the deal?" Taj said. "I love you" she said to him "To the moon and back" he said. He wiped his face with a napkin, "now if you don't' mind, I'd like to get started on desert" he said as he got up and walked over to her side and pulled her chair back. He spread her legs and pulled her thong to the side. He pulled her pussy lips open and began sticking his tongue in and out her pussy. "Damn ma, that shit taste sweet, open wider for daddy" he said. Najah pushed her plate to the side and propped one of her feet on top of the table. "Yeah do that shit" Taj said as he began tongue fucking her. He reached up and began rubbing her large nipples. Najah began to moan, "mmm that feel so good baby" as she watched her man eat the shit out of her pussy. She began moving around in the chair, as she became more aroused. Taj got off his knees and picked her up by her arms and moved the plates and food down to the other side of the table. He pulled off her thongs and turned her around so that she was bent over the table with her ass facing him. "Damn ma, I love your body" Taj said as he took off his pants and boxers and placed his hands on her hips. He began poking his dick against her moist opening. "Papi, dame webo por favor" (give me some dick please). "Don't worry ma, I got you" Taj replied as he stuck his dick deep inside Najah's tight pussy. "Shhhit" Taj groaned as he held onto her hips as he thrust in and out of her pussy. Najah moaned louder, aright fuck me baby." Najah moved one of her hands off the table and put it behind her to spread her ass cheeks so that Taj could go even deeper. The sight of his black dick going in and out of Najah's pussy all creamed up drove Taj crazy. He began to pump faster, "mamie, I want to come in this pussy" he panted, you ready to get urs ma?" he asked Najah. "Yesss, baby, yess" she moaned. They enjoyed the moment as the intensity built up between, and they both exploded in loud yells and moans. Taj pulled out of Najah and sat down in the chair.

He pulled her down on his lap, inhaling the sweet smell of her hair. "I love you mamie" he said. "I love you to Taj . . . all my life" she replied as she hugged him, she couldn't help but think why Taj was keeping the Sin incident from her.

## CHAPTER 79

The next morning, Sin's phone rang he picked it up and looked at the caller id before answering it. Yo" he replied, "oh yeah" he said, he looked over at Monet, who was getting her bags together for the flight to Costa Rica. "Baby leave the bags, one of the men will get that" She looked and smiled at him, "I forgot already" she said rubbing her still flat tummy. "Well I didn't he replied" no lifting shit with my babies in your stomach." "Ok, Ok" she laughed, and went in the other room for a minute. Sin said back into the phone, "alright, I am about to handle something with my girl right now, but just hold shit down til me and Taj get there. Keep them niggers on locked" he whispered into the phone trying to keep Monet from getting wind of anything. "Aight' he said and clicked the phone shut. Monet walked out of the bedroom over to him and gave him a kiss on the lips. "Everything ok baby?" she asked. "Yeah, shit copasetic" he replied as he pulled her close, damn, I about to be a daddy" he said and a nigger bust out twins" he laughed. "Hush yo mouth" Monet laughed and said. "Let's go, we still gotta pick up Taj and Najah too baby. Alight he replied as he clicked his cell open again, Yo ock, we ready to roll, tell Abdul to send somebody in for the bags." he clicked the phone shut. He went in his pocket and peeled off a stack of hundred dollar bills. "Here some money ma, this should hold your ass till me and Taj get down there." He said as someone knocked on the door. One of the security detail came in then waited as Sin and Monet walked towards the front door, there were two guards posted out front, and the 5 of them walked towards the elevators. As they got to the parking level, the security stepped out first and viewed the area to where the cars were parked. They walked to the cars, Sin and Monet walked in between the security detail, as they reached the Mercedes Benz SUV, one of the men opened the doors for Sin and Monet to get in and they headed out of the parking area. A dark colored 4 sedan pulled out behind them slowly. Sin clicked his phone to call Taj, as he lit up a blunt. "Damn! I forgot my baby having babies, this shit gotta go" as he put the blunt back out. "Yo! What's up my nigga", he said into the phone, "we about to be heading you way, we should be there in 30 minutes" he said. "Yeah and I just got a call from Rock, he picked the package up. I told him to wait til we get there to unwrap it." "Alright in a minute, one" he clicked the phone down. "I am a little curious about meeting Najah's family" Monet said, "she has always been so close mouthed about them, these last few years." "I know she and her sister keep in contact, Maria is a few years younger than Najah. She lives with the grandparents, but that's about it" Monet said. Besides being in Costa Rico, baby, I was reading up about the culture and everything there, and it's so beautiful over there" She said. "Yeah, I can't wait til me and Taj get down there after we handle this business, two weeks' vacation, is just what we all need." Sin replied as he pulled Monet into his arms so that she could lean on his chest. He reached down and rubbed her stomach . . . "we going be a real little family ma, me you and the babies, they going to be straight from the door." I don't want him or her to have to worry about nothing in this life." He told her. "I love you baby" Monet said "and your ass better hurry and get down there with me and Najah" "Don't worry, I got you ma, we right behind you" Sin replied as he leaned further back in the seat, thinking about the attempt on his life, the day before. They met Taj and Najah at the landing and waited while the security put the luggage on the private plane. Sin asked Taj did Abdul get back at him with that information. Najah looked at Taj with a confused look. "Nah, not yet" Taj responded. The girls kissed and hugged the men goodbye and boarded the plane to take off.

After the plane had lifted, Taj looked at Sin and said. "Now let's go handle some business." In a darkened storage room in the basement of a small house in Brooklyn, Rahim, aka Detective Rashaun Johnson and a well built white man, with blond hair dressed in slacks, shirt and tie were sitting at a table. The blond man was Rashaun's Lieutenant, Jake Reily.

"How are things going Rashaun? I did get your transmitted report about the one killing initiation that you were forced to participate in." "Any new events that I should be made aware of?" Jake asked Rahim. "Yesterday through the grapevine, there was an attempt made on Sinclair Jones, aka Sin. "There was a drive by attempt, but none of Sin's group was hit." Of course they are taking matters into their hands, so they have street people out, getting answers regarding the attempt on his life." Rahim responded. "Ok Jake replied, I will attempt contact with you again next week, keep your transmits coming through. Here is some extra money to have just to keep up appearances of a well to do gangsta with this "Org" click" he said. "Just keep me abreast and I will talk to you next week" Jake said as he got up from the table and shook Rahim's hand. "Watch your ass out there" he said to Rahim, "I will go out first and you follow after" Later", and he walked out the door. Rahim was supposed to meet Andre, on 125th before heading to the stash house they were assigned to and start the days work. He had failed to tell the lieutenant of how he and Andre smoked that dude that shit deep down, felt good to Rahim, killing just because. He walked over to the door, and looked out, and closed it behind him walked out to the street, looked both ways and jumped in his ride to go meet Andre. He didn't know that Andre had been shot the night before. Meanwhile, the girls had gotten seated in the plush, comfortable seats in the private jet. The plane seated 15 comfortably and had a small staff that cooked whatever was requested by the passengers. There was also a small bar, a pool table, and a large screen TV for movie viewing. The girls ordered breakfast, Najah ordered a moo, moo, a strawberry, bananas, a little mango, orange juice and papaya blended together with ice to make it smoothie, Monet a large cranberry juice. "Girl we are so blessed" said Monet, "we got men who adore us and give us everything we want, we got our own business, and about to start families and shit." Najah, I don't know what I would do if I lost Sin, I mean we riding in private jets and shit, got a purse full of money, but none of these would be shit without him" Now we got the twins coming, girl this is what I always dreamed how my life to be, you know?" Monet said. "Najah took her hand, "I know Monet, we are truly blessed, now let's see what they got up there for some movies and wait and eat our brunch . . . cause we missed a real breakfast" Najah said, "we should arrive there around noon, and someone will be there to pick us up from the airport." "Sounds good" said Monet, I am so greedy girl, I ordered strawberry pancakes, eggs, sausage, and cheese." I know I am going to be huge by the time I am done with pregnancy." Monet laughed. "You're entitled Monet." Najah said. "You will be feeding for three you know" she laughed. "Yeah, you got that right" Monet said as the waiters bought their breakfast to them.

# CHAPTER 80

Sin and Taj had arrived at the warehouse where Rock and some of the other men were waiting. "What's the word my nigga's?" Taj asked. "That nigga tied up in the other room, sweating like a bitch" Rock said. He claiming he don't know nothing." But we also got two witnesses that saw this nigga and two other niggas across town who car was also shot all up, down by the pier, and they recognized Duke." Also, he had $10,000 of the missing loot in lining of his car, with the rest of the money at his mom's crib." Yo, we had to knock that bitch out, she would not give up that money yo!" laughed Rock. "But we didn't kill her."

"Aight! Aight! Let's get down to it said Taj, as he began to walk towards the room where C-Note, was being held. He had been stripped down to his boxers. His arms were chained to grounded brackets in the wall. He had been beaten, there was blood splattered all over him. "We ain't fuck him up to much, Taj." "But nigger was popping mad shit, about how the org only down for themselves and the workers do all the work and get shit, and blah, blah, acting just like a bitch." Rock spat. Sin walked over to a drawer on the side of the room, and pulled out a pair of plastic gloves, he threw a pair to Taj, and he walked over to where C-Note was knocked unconscious. "Nah nigga, it ain't time to sleep" Sin said, he took a blade out his back pocket, and reached down and picked up one of C-Note lifeless fingers, and cut the thumb off. "Yrrrrrrrgggghhh" yelled C-Note waking up out of sub consciousness. He tried to get up off the chair, but he was held and locked by the metal brackets attached to the wall. Sin turned to one of the workers, you give me a seat, I want to seat right here in front of this fat fucks face while he tell me where the rest of our money at." Sin replied. "Its not about the money, it's the principle of him stealing from the hand that fed him." The chair was placed right in front of C-Note huge bleeding body. Sin plopped down in the chair, and stuck a blunt in his mouth. He took a couple of tokes, "I am going ask you this one time where our money at fat boy?" Sin said though a cloud of smoke. Taj and the others stood watching. C-Note, started to talk "Yo Sin, you ain't have to cut my thumb off" C-Note cried out "Shut up nigger" Taj said, $10,000 was found in the trunk of your car, and niggas been talking about you, how you been talking mad shit and just spending our money. "And I suppose you don't know nothing about what happened with somebody trying to get at Sin today either huh?" Taj asked. "Man I was about to bring that shit over to the spot man" C-Note, responded. "I told you before there is rules to this shit nigga." Sin yelled, "and we had to find your ass, so stop lying, motherfucker" he said "Now this is your last chance to talk oh and you should know, we got your moms, and your little sister with some company, and nigga's just waiting for the word, so talk nigga." "Ok! Ok! C-Note said, listen, I been a good soldier for a lot of years, and all I was going to do was bring more money to The Organization I made a connect with these Haitians niggas' "Oh so you making connections moves for us now nigga?"

interrupted Taj, who the fuck do you think you are?" he said. Yo, cut the small talk and get to where the rest of the money at. Taj said. "Alright, alight, I was saying I met one of these dudes and he was talking about getting some weight at a real good price, I mean real good, so I was going to get the info and bring it to ya'll as soon as I got the scoop." C-Note panted, Sin, took his knife and stuck in one of C-Note thighs, and began to slide the knife down towards his knee digging into the flesh. Biggs screamed out loud in pain. "Arrrggg! Wait, it's the truth, it's the truth" he screamed. Sin stood up from the chair in front of C-Note and pushed the chair back. "Nigga you about to be missing." He said as he pulled his gun out, Taj, said, "Nah hold up. we going let the homeys, have fun fucking your moms and sister up the ass. Just because you didn't play your position and tried to take from us. You went and tried to fuck behind our backs and make deals and shit, and this how you've been coming up short the last two weeks." Taj said. "Nah nigga that shit don't add up, so if

THE TAKE DOWN

that's your story, I think its check out time." "Ok, ok" C-Note said, I met dude, this kid named Aaron, his father this big time Haitian cat up in Yonkers, niggas is really popping out there." Nigga wanted to get at us with some good weight at good prices." "They heard about The Organization rep, and wanted fuck with us." "So what instead you tried to make a side deal, off our money right?" interrupted Sin pacing back and forth, he was hot, and very little patience for the shit C-Note was talking. Sin turned to one of the other soldiers in the room with them. "Yo, go get the shit out the other room" he said. "No, no it wasn't like that" C-Note cried out, "please, I was going to bring right to ya'll" he said. Nigga shut up, Sin said turning around, with your lying, stealing ass." So this kid Aaron, where he be at?" he asked C-Note. What Sin and Taj didn't know is that on top of C-Note, making a side deal with the Haitians, he had ripped them off for 8 bricks, making the Haitians think it was The Organization that had ripped them off. "He is over on 145th and St. Nicholas, he got a little spot over there, and a little shawty he fuck with. He is not moving nothing to major, from that location, maybe 25-30g's a week, cause his pops basically running Yonkers on the North and South sides." C-Note replied. The soldier came back in the room, carrying a black burlap bag. C-Note looked at the bag, "Yo, Sin, I told you everything, I was going get that money back to The Organization three times over, yo!" "Save it" Sin said walking over and getting the bag from the worker and walking back in front of where C-Note sat bleeding. He dropped the bag on the floor in front of C-Note s. "You already know what the price for stealing from us, since you were a Lieutenant and all so I ain't even going waste my fucking breath." Sin said as he stood in front of C-Note, I just want you to know that we know that little freak you boning has the rest of the money hidden at her crib." We just wanted to see if you were going to be honest with us and we might have been lenient with your ass." "Think about that, on your way to hell" Sin said as he pointed the gun at C-Note head, and blew his brains all over the wall. Taj looked at two of the silent men in the room, "Dana and Brandon, y'all nigga's take that acid out of the bag, cut this nigga up, and when you're done, pour the acid in his mouth so his body can't be identified by his dental records, and pour the shit on his remaining nine fingers and the one over there on the floor. Dump his body and clean the blood and shit up. He looked at Sin, and said "Did them niggas got the money from the freak's house?" he asked. "Yeah" Sin replied." Sin said. "Hold up I got 20 g's off Biggs and 10 off C-Note, here go your cut nigga." As he handed Taj his cut. Taj looked at Sin and said "we were only short 9. You stupid as they laughed walking towards the door to leave. "Alright, let's go find a nigga name Aaron from Yonkers" he said, as he and Sin walked out the room with their security detail.

# CHAPTER
# 81

Meanwhile, Najah and Monet had arrived in San Jose, Costa Rica's Capital and one of the largest cities there. As the girls came off the private plan, Najah's grandfather was waiting for them with her sister Maria. Najah ran towards them and hugged her sister and grandfather tightly, it had been too long since she had seen them. "Maria, grandfather I am so happy to see you guys" how is everything, where is grand mere?" "Jeez, slow down" Maria laughed, "she is at home" she said, having the staff cook up a feast for you and your guest." Maria said as she looked at Monet, who had walked up behind the three of them. Najah turned around and said, grandfather, Maria this is my friend Monet from New York, she has just found out she is pregnant with twins. "A double blessing" Najah's grandfather said taking Monet's hand and bringing it to his lips. "Hello, nice to meet you."

"I have heard so much about you, I feel like I know you already." Maria said to Monet. "Come" said Najah's grandfather, whose name was Antonio, let's get back to the house. Dinner will be served at 8:00. They all walked towards the awaiting Hummer limo. The security detail put the luggage in the back and they drove off. As they traveled through the city, Monet said 'it's so beautiful here" she sighed. "Later on Maria and Najah why don't you take your friend on a tour of the city." Antonio said. "Sounds good to me the girls said as they pulled up to the large colonial styled mansion, they walked into a beautifully decorated house. And a fashionably dressed woman with black hair pulled up into a bun came into the foyer. She wore small diamond earrings in her ears, and she wore few pieces of very expensive jewelry around her neck and arms. "Grandmother, Najah said as she hugged the woman, how are you, I am so happy to see you" Her grandmother smiled, she was still a very beautiful woman for her age. "And you must be Monet" she said looking at Monet. She gave her a hug, "welcome to our home. Why don't you girls go and get freshened up and unpacked and I will see you down stairs shortly." Annabella said. "Ok Abuela" Najah said, come on Monet I will show you to your room, the staff will bring the bags up for us." Maria, are you coming up with us so we can get caught up before dinner?" "Sure I will be up in a minute." Maria replied I have a phone call to return" she said. "Ok see you upstairs."

# CHAPTER 82

After the girls had freshened up and got un-packed, they went downstairs and had dinner. Antonio keeps them all laughing with his funny stories and jokes. After dinner before the girls were set to go and show Monet the city, which was beautiful at night. Antonio asked one of the servants to bring Najah to his study. She walked in her grandfather was sitting behind his large desk, smoking an expensive cigar. "Have a seat Najah Marie" he said. She knew when he called her by her full name it was something serious he wanted to speak with her about. "So when were you going to tell me about the attack on you at your house?" he asked, she knew her grandfather had eyes and ears everywhere. She told him what happened and including the weird tattoos the men hand on the back of their hands, which was a green dragon with red eyes and some sort of family crest symbol. Antonio frowned when she described the tattoo. "Yes, I know that symbol" he said, I already have the men on it, but something else has come to my attention Najah. The man that had your parents killed, I found out that he was called Black Ty, and had a son that took over his business for him." "A son, that none of us knew of, apparently the boy was kept hidden till now. The boy has an unusual name Sincere David, he is known as Sin in the street. This man is also the partner of your fiancée Taj. This might be a problem Meha, because Sin has to die for the death of your parents. Najah felt the room close in, and everything went black . . .